It's New Year's 1 hearts

When a woman with no faith in love meets the quintessential nice guy determined to breach her mile-high walls, sparks fly as both fight a decidedly unwelcome but equally unavoidable attraction.

Steph Hargrove was a bombshell, a sexy, intrepid woman operating in the business world with guts, brains and daring. She was accustomed to going after whatever she wanted until a man she called friend betrayed her and the company she'd helped build—and nearly killed her in the process. Since that time, she's been a shadow of the wild, wicked woman who'd carved a swath through her world.

Gavin O'Neill is an artisan with wood, a gardener, a restorer of battered homes and a savior of strays. When first he meets the wounded woman who postures as invincible and worldly, the sadness in her eyes draws him even more than her lush figure does. However she insists otherwise, he sees that she needs the kindness and friendship he can give that to her while he's waiting for the woman of his dreams, who will be small and soft and sweet, different in every way from the woman he keeps returning to see.

Yet while he's not interested in the virago and she refuses to be nurtured, a potent attraction keeps them circling each other. And while they're busy listing the reasons they're unsuited, something powerful is growing between them.

New Year's Eve is for lovers and new beginnings…will these two stubborn souls take the risk?

BOOKS BY JEAN BRASHEAR

SWEETGRASS SPRINGS:
Texas Roots
Texas Wild
Texas Dreams
Texas Rebel
Texas Blaze
Texas Christmas Bride
The Book Babes

Texas Hope
Texas Strong
Texas Sweet
Be Mine This Christmas
Texas Charm
Texas Magic
Be My Midnight Kiss
Cooking Kissing and Cowboys

THE GALLAGHERS OF MORNING STAR
(cousins of the Sweetgrass Springs clan)
Texas Secrets
Texas Lonely
Texas Bad Boy

LONE STAR LOVERS
Texas Heartthrob
Texas Healer
Texas Protector
Texas Deception
Texas Lost
Texas Wanderer
Texas Bodyguard
Texas Rescue

THE MARSHALLS
Texas Refuge
Texas Star
Texas Danger

SECOND CHANCES series
Guarding Gaby
Bringing Bella Back
The Price He Paid
The House That Love Built
The Road Back Home
Mercy
Dream House

STANDALONE Romances
The Light Walker
The Choice

WOMEN'S FICTION
The Goddess of Fried Okra

Be My Midnight Kiss

**Sweetgrass Springs
Book Fourteen**

Jean Brashear

Copyright © 2017 Jean Brashear
Print Edition

This is a work of fiction. Names, characters, places and incidents are either the product of the author's imagination or are used fictitiously, and any resemblance to actual persons, living or dead, business establishments, events or locales is entirely coincidental.

© Covers by Stacy Stephens

Formatting by BB eBooks:
bbebooksthailand.com

Dedication

I can't begin to thank you enough, all of you lovely readers who want to return with me to Sweetgrass Springs each time! Your enthusiasm for this little town and the time we all spend there is such a blessing. Thank you for every review you write, every note you send me, every comment or like or share—they may not be that big a deal to you, but I promise you they mean the world to me!

I am so grateful for each and every one of you for the trust you express each time you choose to try another of my stories. It's an honor and a privilege I never take for granted.

So this one's for you, all you Sweetgrass Springs lovers. May the spirit of this town where hope never fades and love never dies give your own hearts some of the same joy and respite it gives mine.

And, always and forever, for Ercel, for more reasons than the number of stars in the sky.

The Families of Sweetgrass Springs

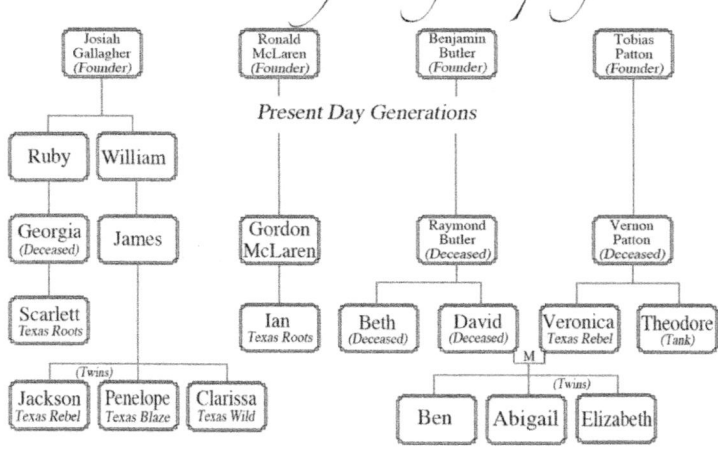

The Gallaghers

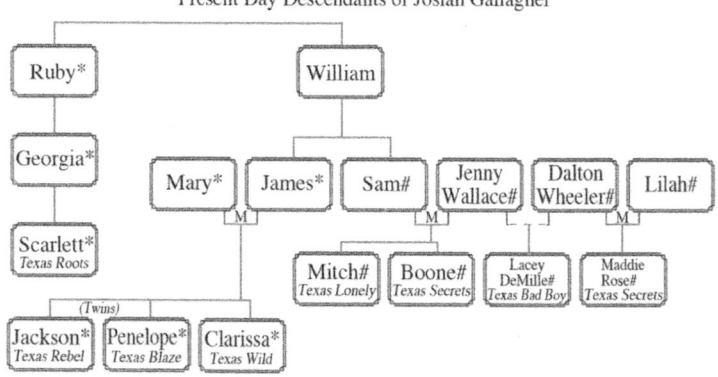

[M] = Married
[_ _ _] = Affair
* = Gallaghers of Sweetgrass Springs
\# = Gallaghers of Morning Star

SWEETGRASS SPRINGS
Cast of Characters
(titles in parentheses mark a character's primary story)

THE FOUR FOUNDING FAMILIES:

THE GALLAGHERS
(Josiah Gallagher, Sweetgrass Springs founder)

Ruby Gallagher – diner owner and the heart and soul of this struggling small town

James Gallagher – Ruby's brother and father of twins Jackson and Penny plus Rissa.

Scarlett Ross – Ruby's granddaughter, New York chef whose deceased mother Georgia never told her they had family in Texas (*Texas Roots, Texas Dreams*)

Jackson Gallagher – video game tycoon and prodigal son of James who's been missing for twenty years (*Texas Rebel, Texas Christmas Bride*)

Penelope Gallagher – Jackson's twin sister, shark lawyer who left Sweetgrass Springs behind (*Texas Blaze, Texas Christmas Bride*)

Clarissa Gallagher – youngest child of James and horse whisperer; the only one of James's children who cares about the ranch (*Texas Wild*)

THE MCLARENS
(Ronald McLaren, Sweetgrass Springs founder)

Gordon McLaren – owner of the Double Bar M Ranch with his son Ian (*Texas Hope*)

Ian McLaren – Gordon's son whose mother abandoned him

as a child; now runs Double Bar M Ranch. Unofficial mayor of Sweetgrass Springs and its mainstay alongside Ruby (*Texas Roots, Texas Dreams*)

Sophia McLaren Cavanaugh – the mother Ian has never forgiven for leaving him behind (*Texas Hope*)

Michael Cavanaugh – Ian's half-brother by Sophia's second husband. Neither Michael nor Ian was ever told the other exists (*The Book Babes, Texas Hope*)

THE PATTONS
(Tobias Patton, Sweetgrass Springs founder)

Vernon Patton – deceased, abusive father of Veronica and Theodore (Tank)

Veronica Patton Butler – Jackson Gallagher's teenage sweetheart left behind when he vanished. She married Jackson's close friend David Butler. Owner of a flower farm and David's widow (*Texas Rebel, Texas Christmas Bride*)

Theodore "Tank" Patton – deputy sheriff and the most reviled man in Sweetgrass Springs (*Texas Hope*)

THE BUTLERS
(Benjamin Butler, Sweetgrass Springs founder)

Raymond Butler – deceased father of David Butler

David Butler – one of the most beloved citizens of Sweetgrass Springs. High school buddies with Jackson Gallagher, Ian McLaren and Randall Mackey. Died leaving his widow Veronica with a son Ben and twins Abby and Beth.

Beth Butler – David's sister who died in the car accident that caused Jackson Gallagher to be banished

OTHER IMPORTANT SWEETGRASS SPRINGS CHARACTERS:

Randall Mackey, close friend of Ian McLaren, Jackson Gallagher and David Butler. Joined the Navy after high school; became a SEAL. After leaving the service, wound up as a stuntman in Hollywood (*Texas Wild*)

Bridger Calhoun, former SEAL buddy of Mackey's, now a firefighter (*Texas Blaze, Texas Christmas Bride*)

Harley Sykes (wife Melba, a quilter) – one of the coffee group that meets every morning at Ruby's. One of the town's most colorful characters.

Raymond Benefield (wife Nita, also a quilter) – one of the coffee group regulars.

Arnie Howard – coffee group regular at Ruby's who's been warming Ruby's bed for many years but can never convince her to marry him

Jeanette Carson – sharp-tongued veteran waitress at Ruby's. Attended high school a few years behind Ian McLaren, for whom she's been carrying a torch for years (*Texas Charm*)

Brenda Jones – skittish teenaged waitress at Ruby's who just showed up in Sweetgrass one day and has secrets she keeps (*Texas Sweet*)

Henry Jansen – busboy turned cook at Ruby's; young man whose chivalry towards Brenda turns to blushes when noticed (*Texas Sweet*)

Spike Ridley – tattooed Goth pastry chef with an attitude; her skills are unparalleled, but her motto might as well be "have mixer will travel."

Walker Roundtree – country music superstar; spars with Jeanette and performs at several Sweetgrass weddings (*Texas Charm*)

Chapter One

Austin, Texas

Laken Foster arrived at the storefront beneath Stephanie Hargrove's downtown loft and buzzed to be let in.

"Come on up." Steph unlocked her door as her energetic friend moved up the stairs at less than her usual warp speed.

"There are perfectly great condos with elevators all over downtown now," Laken pointed out.

Steph shrugged. "This works for me."

"Are you really glad you moved to Austin? Everyone in Sweetgrass misses you."

"That's nice to hear." But she didn't want to discuss the matter. It was not the fault of the good people of that tiny town that she felt more alone surrounded by all the loving couples, all the romance she'd never be part of, than when she was all by herself. "I'll get my purse. Want me to drive to book club?" She'd been invited to join Laken's reading group, the Book Babes, and appreciated the new friends she'd made.

"Nah. My car is parked illegally a block away. Let's make tracks before I get a ticket."

"Or towed. You know how downtown works."

"My place in SoCo didn't have garage space either. I learned to be pretty creative about finding street parking."

"You miss living in the city."

"No, of course not—" Laken exhaled in a gust. "Not exactly. Michael isn't in Sweetgrass, and I don't want to be without him."

"He'd move for you."

"He would, but his veterinary practice is in the country. He loves it there. Sweetgrass is too far to commute, and he gets called out at all hours."

"But you could telecommute from here, too. You know Jackson would let you." They both worked for Enigma Games, Jackson Gallagher's enormously successful video gaming company. Laken had come onboard as in-house counsel after falling in love with Michael Cavanaugh, while Steph had been with Enigma since its early days in Seattle.

She'd been betrayed there. Nearly died there. Had trusted the wrong man and been frozen ever since.

She'd thought she was finished at Jackson's company, certain that her bad judgment couldn't be forgiven, but Jackson Gallagher was as loyal to his people as they were to him. He'd given her a long sabbatical to recover but insisted her marketing skills made her indispensable to Enigma.

Laken glanced away. "We're not talking about me. How come you left, really? Did something happen?"

"Nothing happened. The city suits me better. I don't need to be in the office with Jackson that often, anyway. I've actually thought about returning to Seattle. As long as I have internet, I can handle my job from anywhere…"

"But—?"

"Seattle has a lot of memories I'm not sure I'm ready to face, but I also don't really fit the Sweetgrass lifestyle. All those ridiculously happy couples—" Abruptly she registered Laken's unhappy expression. "Wait—is something going on with you and Michael?" However envious she was of all those couples so deeply in love, she wouldn't wish strife on any of them. Some of them, like Jackson himself, had suffered greatly before finding love.

An odd expression flitted over Laken's features. "Something's going on, all right," she muttered.

Abruptly she went pale and clutched her stomach. She grabbed Steph's arm. "Sorry—" She raced for the bathroom and slammed the door.

From behind it came the unmistakable sounds of retching.

Swell. Laken was sick and was going to share the wealth. Steph willed her own too-sympathetic stomach not to join the club. After several deep breaths, she approached the door. "Want me to call Michael or take you to an urgent care clinic or—"

"No!" A flush. Water running. The door opened and a panicky Laken tried to smile. "Don't. Please. I'll be fine—"

Abruptly her face took on a nasty greenish cast. She slammed the door again.

Where is my hand sanitizer? Steph was reaching for her phone while looking for a bottle. She searched for Michael on her phone contacts.

The door opened again. "You don't need to call anyone," Laken said, sagging against the door.

"Of course I do. Michael would want to know, and I'll call the group to tell them we aren't going to make it. We're driving to get you help first—"

"I'm beyond help."

Steph's mind went wild with frightening suppositions—

Until she realized Laken was smiling.

Then abruptly her friend's eyes filled with tears. "I'm not sick. I'm...pregnant." She tried to smile again, but instead her face crumpled. "I'm..." She closed her eyes. "Pregnant." Her hand covered her mouth.

Steph's brows rose. "But it's evening. Morning sickness—"

"Leave it to me to do it all ass-backwards. I'm just dandy in the mornings and most all day. I don't know if Junior here is a night owl or simply perverse." She laid a hand on her stomach, a few more tears spilling over.

Yet there was wonder shining through the fear.

Steph couldn't tell how she should respond. "Um...congratulations?"

Sunny once more, Laken chuckled. "Call Michael with those. He's over the moon and insanely happy—or he would be if I'd just marry him."

They'd been together for two years, and Michael had made no bones of the fact that he wanted them to be together forever. Laken was the roadblock to making their bond permanent. "You're not happy about this? You—of course you know there are options."

"Not for me. Living with a man who's devoted his life to saving every furry species on earth? Who would sell his soul for me to help him repopulate the earth all by ourselves?"

"But if you don't want this baby—"

Laken's eyes were stark with both fear and longing. "I want it more than I've ever wanted anything in my life." Brusquely she scrubbed at her wet cheeks. "But what do I know about being a mother? My parents have been divorced forever, and I mostly raised myself. Michael's baby deserves the best mom in the world, and I—I'm not—I can't—I don't know how to—"

Steph froze in place. What was she supposed to say to make things better? Her own mother had chosen the sweet surrender of drugs over her daughter. She knew less than Laken did about good mothering.

Laken shoved to standing. "And listen to me, whiney-babying it. I'm the luckiest woman ever that Michael lost his mind and fell in love with me. Heaven knows he could raise this baby singlehanded. He'll be the best dad in the world but me, I—" She sank to the sofa. "I don't know if I can do this. And I don't want to go see Earth Mother Ellie tonight because she'll tell me how easy it all is, how you just have to love them and love their father and everything will be fine." She shook her head. "I've barely figured out how to take care of the dog Michael gave me. Plus everyone in Sweetgrass will be watching me and they're all like Ellie, such amazing mothers, but I'm going to do everything wrong. I just know it."

Wow. Steph wanted to help this woman who was a kindred spirit, who'd become such a good friend, but Steph understood Laken's fears only too well. Some women weren't meant to be mothers. Her own had been one of them, and Steph was no different.

Laken did, however, have the best man in the world at her side.

Right now, though, Laken wouldn't want Michael's easy assurance because Michael couldn't understand. He'd never doubted his own ability to love, but she knew from conversations with Laken that her friend and she shared that essential awareness of the lack in themselves.

"Penny didn't want to get married or have babies, but look at her. She's an awesome mom to JJ."

"Yeah, she was a shark lawyer like me, but at least she grew up in Sweetgrass. Her parents loved each other until the day her mother died, and her father still hasn't gotten over losing Mary. Plus Penny has Bridger."

Steph understood. "Bridger and Michael are a lot alike. They're both healers. Nurturers." And seriously hot. Some women had it all.

"Penny belongs there. I don't. I could have left and gone back to my life until this happened. I always figured one day Michael would tire of my BS, and we'd just...part ways. Remain good friends."

Steph snorted. "Seriously?"

"No, of course not. I was never going to be nice about splitting up. I'd be boiling bunnies."

Steph laughed, and Laken chuckled.

Then her face crumpled again. "But now—" Her face was a study in misery. "We'll be tied together forever, and I don't want him to be with me because of this child. I've been that kid, living in a house filled with hard feelings. And the all-out battles over custody—"

"Laken, get a grip. You're barely pregnant, and you're already in family court. You love Michael, right?" She huffed. "Why do I ask? You're crackers crazy over the guy, and he's so gone on you, little hearts and cupids practically swirl around his head when he looks at you. You're not heading for a divorce."

"Because we're not married yet," Laken wailed.

"Good grief. I'm not going to bitch-slap the pregnant lady," Steph muttered. But somebody had to talk Laken off the ledge. She desperately wanted to call Laken's closest friend, Ava Sinclair. Ava would know how to handle Laken.

She just had to get Laken to book club, so Ava could take over. The five Book Babes had been friends for years.

"Here." She shoved a handful of tissues in front of Laken. "Go wash your face so we can rescue your car. Let's swap it for mine, and I'll drive."

"I don't think I want to go," Laken said from behind her tissue.

Tough love was all Steph could figure out as a fix. Laken was generally exceedingly logical. If this was pregnancy, Steph could only thank her lucky stars she'd never caught the malady. "The alternative is that I call Michael."

Laken glared. "You suck." There was little heat in the insult, though.

Steph filled a glass with water and took it to her.

Laken rolled her eyes and sighed. "You were supposed to pity me. And find me a way out."

"You don't want a way out. You love that man to distraction. Anyway, you'd bite my head off if I tried to pity you."

"Once, sure. Maybe I'm different now."

Steph snorted. "Yeah. You've added self-pity to your badass repertoire. It doesn't fit all that well, girlfriend. Do Sophia and Gordon know they're about to be grandparents again?"

"Nobody knows. It's making Michael miserable not to be able to tell even his brother Ian. The two of them are thick as thieves now. Ian has taken to fatherhood like a duck to water, and Michael can't wait to join him."

"Well, your secret's out, and I'm not keeping it for you. You're tougher than this, Laken. When's the wedding?"

Laken groaned. "Yesterday, if Michael had his way. I should have never gotten involved with a man who loves animals and babies," she muttered.

"I think that horse, as Ruby would say, is out of the barn." Steph smirked because she knew Laken would take insult better than pity. "Now get off your soon-to-be-massive behind or we'll be late."

Laken glared, her old spirit returning. "Have I told you lately that you stink as a girlfriend?"

"Move it. Just because you're knocked up is no excuse for being rude. Besides, this is great news."

"How can you say that?" For a second, Laken's smile trembled.

"Because." Steph cast an evil grin on her friend. "I get your share of the wine for months and months and months."

"You're a cold-hearted bitch, you know that?" But Laken was smiling again.

"I know. That's why you like me." Steph ushered her friend out the door, breathing a sigh of relief that she would soon have reinforcements.

"So have you met any hot guys we need to hear about?" Ava Sinclair asked Steph as the four of them present tonight got settled with wine. Two members were missing: Sylvie and her Gabe were in Europe scouting new talent for Sylvie's art gallery and Luisa and her son Carlos were on a college-hunting trip.

Only Laken didn't have a glass. She'd used an early-morning conference call as an excuse, then glared at Steph to remain silent about the real reason.

"I'm not in the market right now." Steph responded after making a *get-on-with-it* face at Laken.

Laken stared right back, and Steph stifled an eye-roll. She wished Laken would go ahead and tell them and take the heat off her, but...Laken would be Laken.

"Why not?" Ava asked. "You're single and gorgeous, newly moved from the back of beyond. Austin is full of eligible men, and I'm pretty sure you haven't taken a vow of celibacy."

Ava would be surprised. Yes, Steph used to troll the waters, spending a fortune on clothes and stilettos to display her bombshell body, streaking her black hair with red for maximum impact, working out obsessively to keep her figure as she cut a swath through the men in her path and discarded them just as quickly.

But that was the old Steph, the one who hadn't nearly died. She wasn't sure who the new Steph was.

"Ava..." Ellie Preston, their hostess tonight, eased between them, a fresh wine bottle in hand. "Don't badger Steph. You'll hurt her feelings. More wine?"

"Hard-nosed executives don't have feelings, sweetie." Ava grinned at Steph.

Steph snickered.

"Anyway, how are we old married ladies supposed to live vicariously through her if she plays her cards close to the vest?" Ava asked. "Don't let us down, Steph."

"It's her business," Ellie protested, "and she doesn't have to share the details of her sex life...unless she wants to?" Her eyebrows rose at the end of the sentence, along with her voice.

Steph laughed and so did Laken. Even after five kids and a serious marital crisis, Earth Mother Ellie still possessed an innocent air that life couldn't seem to erase. The room around them reflected her nurturing tendencies: bright splashes of color, soft cushions she'd upholstered, candles made by hand, needlework and thriving plants everywhere.

"I've been settling in. I'll get around to it."

Ava snorted. "Seriously? When you're surrounded by all the eye candy?"

Truth to tell, she'd barely noticed. She'd stayed in her loft and…worked. Read books. Worked some more. She was pathetic. Ava was right. She did need to get back on the horse.

"I know someone you need to meet," Ellie piped up. "There's this amazing carpenter who works for Wyatt, Gavin O'Neill. He's—"

Steph flashed her palm. "Stop right there. Don't even think about matchmaking." She rested her head on one fist. "If only real men were like the ones you write in your romance novels, Ava."

"You'd never let them be the alpha male, girlfriend."

"Stop teasing her, Ava." Ellie turned to Steph. "Gavin's special. You'll meet him at Thanksgiving."

"You're going to Ellie's gathering of lost souls at Thanksgiving?" Laken asked. "I'd hoped you'd join us. Ian and Scarlett and Ruby and Arnie are coming to our place this year."

And they'd be celebrating the baby. Plus a wedding. No thank you. "Jackson and Veronica invited me, too, but—"

"We've got dibs on her, Laken. You don't mind, do you?"

Steph didn't care if Laken did mind. She was happy to have an excuse not to be in Sweetgrass to compare the state of her life to all those around her. Even cranky Jeanette, the former waitress from Ruby's café, had found her happily-ever-after with, of all people, country music superstar Walker Roundtree. She had an instant daughter in Walker's orphaned niece Maisie, and she was already pregnant with his child. All that, and she'd started her own business on the town square, which was already doing very well.

But Steph was not up for Ellie's matchmaking. "Ellie, that's not why I'm coming. I don't want to be anyone's blind date."

"It's not a blind date, it's a gathering of friends."

Lost souls, Laken mouthed, flashing an L sign with her hand. *Losers like you.*

Watch it, or I'll squeal, Steph mouthed back.

Laken shut up.

Steph returned her attention to Ellie. "Look, I know you mean well. I'm just not—that's not what I want. I'm fine like I am." She glanced desperately at Laken.

Laken was only too aware that she had the perfect conversation-switcher. But she wasn't ready to admit—

What? Who was she fooling? She loved Michael with her last breath. The mere thought of life without him was unbearable.

And having a baby with him was nearly as thrilling as it was terrifying.

"Enough about Steph." She cleared her throat. "I have news that tops anything of hers."

Steph looked like she wanted to hug her.

"Oh?" Ava turned her attention from Steph.

Ellie sat up straighter. "You and Michael are getting married!" She clapped her hands, then laughed. "Oh, dear. Should Sylvie get ready for the red and gold ruffles?" Once Laken had tormented their very stylish friend about making her attendants, especially the dignified Sylvie, wear flamenco dresses.

Laken's bravado faltered. "Maybe. Probably. I don't know."

"What's wrong, sweetie?" Ellie rose and started over.

Laken held up a hand. "Don't. Please. I—sympathy will only—" She looked at Steph. "I can't say it. You tell them."

"Tell us what? Oh, no—is something wrong?"

Steph smirked. "Only if you're Laken. She has an amazing man crazy in love with her and she's carrying his baby."

Ava laughed uproariously.

Ellie shot Ava a glare. "Why on earth would you laugh?"

Ava was shaking her head but still chuckling.

Laken sighed. "Because she knows my goose is cooked. Michael is, as you can imagine, over the moon about the baby. And not about to let me stall any longer on getting married."

"Good for him." Ellie nodded. "I have never been able to understand why you've dragged your feet." Her brow wrinkled. "Are you unhappy about the baby, is that it?" Clearly the thought troubled her.

"You mean because I'll be the world's worst mother?" Dread filled her. Tears burned her eyes. "What am I going to do?" she whispered. "I'll be awful."

Ellie was by her side in an instant, an arm around her shoulders. "You will not. You're wonderful with my kids."

"Because they're not mine. I can't ruin them. Anyway, we just play. There's so much more than play to raising a child. Michael is this baby's only hope. Maybe I'm doing him an injustice if I marry him." Her faith in the institution of marriage was minimal at best. Her parents had delighted in making her the rope in their constant tug of war, and the best day of her life had been when they'd parted just before she turned eight. Not that they didn't still use her as a weapon, but they'd moved to opposite coasts and now that she was grown, she could dodge them fairly easily most of the time.

Some people were meant for the vine-covered cottage, the puppies and kittens and babies.

She was not one of them.

Other people got married because they couldn't stand being alone. She had been fine on her own. She'd liked living on the edge, keeping her options open. Staying light on her feet.

No shackles for her.

Then along had come Michael Cavanaugh, with his big heart and strong shoulders—and the blasted man had made her love him. Made it so that she could never be happy again without him.

Ellie patting her shoulder was well-meant but wasn't helping. Steph looked completely out of her league.

Laken looked across at Ava. "Well, aren't you going to say anything?"

"Yeah. Stop being a drama queen."

Ellie gasped. "Ava!"

At last Laken laughed. "Bitch. How come I like you so much?"

"Because I'm the only one who calls you on your BS." Ava grinned. "You think you'll be finished with your pity party anytime soon?"

"Maybe you should take my concerns seriously." Laken pouted.

Ava snorted. "Not a chance. Michael's the best thing that ever happened to you, and you know it. You've been leading him on a merry dance and now you're caught. What are you planning to do about it?"

Laken stuck out her tongue. "Let Ellie pet me and make me feel better."

"Michael's already pampering you too much. Get over yourself. That baby does deserve the best mother, so you're going to have to get used to living in fear like the rest of us."

Laken frowned. "You're never afraid. And Ellie is the perfect mom."

Ava and Ellie traded glances loaded with meaning.

Then Ellie patted her shoulder and rose. "Motherhood is a constant rollercoaster of uncertainty, punctuated by terror, interrupted by brief moments of rapturous peace." Her grin was filled with mischief. "Very brief."

"And you did this five times? On purpose?"

Ellie's smile was filled with joy. "I'd do it again in a heartbeat. How about you, Ava?"

Ava's eyes went soft. "Mine are grown, but...yes. In a heartbeat."

Laken looked at Steph, who was shaking her head, mystified as Laken was.

"You people are crazy. Anyone want to talk about the book?"

Everyone laughed.

"Nope. Time to plan a wedding. And a baby shower—yippee!" Ellie's eyes glowed.

Laken rolled her eyes but thanked her lucky stars for her friends.

Gavin O'Neill rose with the chickens.

Literally. His rooster was a walking alarm clock.

The far East Austin neighborhood where he lived was an old one with large lots and a country feel to it. Plenty of room for his big garden, his chicken coop and the woodworking shop he'd made from a detached garage that had—like the house—been close to falling down when he'd bought the place for a song.

And one day, room for a whole pack of children.

His family still hoped he'd return to Tennessee, settle down with a nice country girl and raise a large family as most of his siblings were doing. He'd had the same intention once, that after he'd traveled the U.S. and satisfied his wanderlust, he'd return home only months after he'd left.

That had been seven years ago. Instead he'd found Texas, a big, rowdy state that suited him like a second skin. He missed his family, yes, but he'd found home. Not The Woman yet, no, but that would come in time. He hadn't finished the house in which he and she would raise babies, but he could picture her, nonetheless. She'd have curves, real ones, that gave a man whole handfuls of woman to love. She'd bake bread, sew, garden with him, appreciate the simple life and be a good partner to him. No, he wasn't a throwback as some of his friends accused—he would appreciate and support her career if she had one, could teach her to bake bread if she didn't know how or make it himself as he currently did. They would share values, however, and that would make all the difference—any rough edges could be smoothed out.

He was looking for an Ellie, really. Wyatt Preston, the builder for whom he subcontracted trim carpentry, was married to the woman of Gavin's dreams, the perfect mother and wife who had created a refuge where Wyatt could retreat at the end of a long day.

Too bad she was taken, he thought, smiling. Ellie swore she was going to find the right woman for him, and he'd gladly accept her help. He believed in his heart the woman of his dreams was out there somewhere.

He simply had to be patient.

He was nothing if not a patient man.

Michael Cavanaugh limped into the kitchen of the old farmhouse where his half-brother Ian's great-grandparents had lived. The mare who'd been foaling in his brother's barn tonight had taken issue with Michael's hands being where she hadn't wanted them, and he hadn't moved quite quickly enough to escape the hoof she'd used to demonstrate her displeasure.

It was hardly the first time he'd been injured on the job, and tonight he almost didn't care that he'd have a bruise the size of a grapefruit on his right thigh.

Because this foal belonged to him. He was still shaking his head over Ian's announcement as they'd proudly watched the little guy get to his feet for the first time.

"You can't—" He'd been honestly dumbfounded.

"Did you lie to me when you said you'd like to join me in the horse-breeding business?" Ian had asked.

"No, but—"

"Is this mare mine to do with as I please?"

"Sure, but—"

"Look, I know I was a total jerk to you when you first showed up, but we're past that now. Ugly as you might be, I'm getting used to having a brother, and you being a built-in veterinarian for my stables—our stables—seems like a pretty good deal."

Michael snickered at the sibling abuse, then sobered. "You've built all this yourself." Ian was a cattle rancher, but horses were his first love.

"Ever since you came, you've refused to charge me for visits. I'd say that constitutes an investment."

"But—"

"Do you want this or not?"

Michael had never been an idiot. Well, except for his total inability to walk away from Laken Foster, troublesome as she was, resistant to the life he was determined to build with her. "Hell, yes, I want this. Ian—" He'd raked his fingers through his hair, then stuck out his hand. "I have some money saved up."

"Save it for your never-ending home improvement project. I'm telling you, you should have built from scratch like Scarlett and I did." The couple had built their own home on Ian's favorite spot on the Double Bar M Ranch, leaving the house where Ian had been raised for his father Gordon and their mother Sophia to have privacy, now that the two had been reunited so many years after Sophia had left Gordon and Ian behind.

Michael could still recall his shock and fury that his mother had had a whole life before him, one that included this brother he'd never known about.

But all that was water under the bridge now. The road to healing hadn't been smooth, particularly for Ian and their mother, but Gordon's insistence on taking the lion's share of the blame for the long-ago parting had finally worn through Ian's resistance like water on rock.

The reconciliation had been aided and abetted by the deep love their mom bore for her first son. Her love had been shadowed by guilt and grief for so many years, but the birth of Ian's first child, Georgia Sophia, had forged a link that grew stronger by the day.

"I'll get the house finished one of these days. If we're going to be partners, I want to know I've contributed."

"You'll be a hundred and four by the time you get through teaching Laken basic carpentry skills." Ian had grinned to show that he was teasing.

He wasn't wrong, but Laken deserved credit. She was an enthusiastic if low-skilled worker. Scraping old paint off woodwork, sanding old pine floors, peeling off wallpaper—none of those fit into her previous lifestyle of mani-pedis, stilettos, random hookups and clubbing. But oddly, she seemed to want the roots of the home's history as much as he did.

I don't want her doing manual labor anymore, though, he had wanted to say. He'd wanted so badly to share his news with his brother, to tell Ian he was to be a father, too. He knew he would be a good one and man, he was so ready. After a lifetime of being an only child, he wanted all the family he could get.

But Laken wasn't ready, just as she wasn't ready to marry him.

If he hadn't dealt with skittish animals for so many years, his patience would have flat run out. His Laken—and damn it, she was his, ring or no ring—was more nervy than any of them.

The back door creaked open, and suddenly, there she was.

"Hi," she said.

"Hi, yourself." He dried his hands and turned to her just as she caught his mouth in a heated kiss.

Not being a stupid man, he didn't waste any time, yanking her closer, tilting his head to deepen the kiss. She wrapped her arms around his neck and plastered her body all along his. He forgot all about his bruised leg in the heat of how much he wanted her. That never changed, except to deepen, to grow stronger.

If he could just be patient a little longer, maybe...

Abruptly, Laken broke the kiss, breathing hard and staring intently at him.

"What is it?"

She closed her eyes and glanced away. His heart sank. Lately she'd been hot and cold with him, and he was trying not to lose faith that what they had would prove strong enough to overcome all her doubts.

Give her a break. Don't pressure her.

He swallowed his pride once more and let go of the topic that troubled them both. For different reasons.

"Guess what Ian did tonight—"

"Okay, let's tell Ian and Scarlett and your mom and Gordon—" she spoke at the same moment.

He blinked.

"Wait, what did Ian do?" she asked.

He kept himself very still. Didn't let hope soar. "Tell them what?"

She flushed. Cast her eyes down. "You know. About the baby and—"

He was almost afraid to breathe. "And what?"

When she glanced up, her eyes were shy. His bold, brassy Laken—shy. "And..." Then it was she who swallowed hard.

Took a deep breath before continuing in a rush. "And oh my god I hope you won't regret this and I'm terrified you will, but do you still want to get married?"

It took him a minute to believe his ears. "Seriously?" His voice was barely a whisper.

Her eyes filled with tears. Her fingers stroked his face. "My poor Michael. What have I done to you, you patient and too-kind man?"

He laid his hand over hers and closed his eyes. "I am surely the happiest man in the world right now. The love of my life is going to marry me and have my baby and—" His eyes popped open and he lifted her in his arms, then twirled her in a circle "—and we have a horse!"

She started laughing while Ajax danced around their feet, barking and wanting to join the fun. "We have a what?"

He wrapped her up so tightly he wondered if she could breathe, but surely she could if she was laughing and—

Suddenly, he had everything he'd ever wanted, and his knees went week. "I have to sit down. You have to sit down. How are you feeling? Are you okay?"

She shoved him into the closest kitchen chair, then climbed right onto his lap, covering his face with kisses. "No, I'm scared spitless and I still think you're insane for wanting to load yourself down with me, but—" She grinned hugely. "Too late now, sucker." She threw out her arms, nearly toppling backwards before he caught her. She grabbed on tightly and whooped. "We're both insane, but guess what, Ajax? We're getting married and we have a baby and a puppy and a—" She glanced at Michael. "Seriously? We have a horse?"

"A foal. He was just born tonight."

"And why exactly do we have a baby horse?"

"Ian gave him to me. He wants to be partners in the breeding operation."

"For real?" She was smiling.

"I still can't believe it."

"I can. Ian isn't stupid. You two will be amazing together. You already are." She bent to Ajax. "So you're not our only baby now, and you'll just have to deal, young man." Then she rose and turned to Michael. "Let's go tell Ian thank you and that he's going to be an uncle and we're going to—holy crap!"

Abruptly she was the one who sat down. Then put her head between her knees. "I'm getting married. And having a baby. Michael, what have you done?" she wailed.

Michael laughed and crouched beside her, rubbing her back. "Just breathe, babe. It's gonna be fine. Actually, everything's going to be amazing. Want to get married tomorrow?"

Laken moaned.

Michael just kept smiling.

Chapter Two

Steph nearly hadn't come to the Preston Thanksgiving, but she was sick of her own company. She'd gone from a town too interested in her well-being to being surrounded by strangers in Austin. That she felt the slightest bit lonely was unnerving, though. She'd been on her own most of her life.

She didn't know much about traditional family Thanksgivings besides what she'd seen on TV, but Ellie's would be less overwhelming, surely, than being in Sweetgrass Springs.

So…Thanksgiving for Ellie's Losers. Ellie spotted her as she parked in a location that would make it easy for her to leave, so she'd have to go inside now. She wouldn't be rude to one of the sweetest souls she'd ever met.

She was a lousy cook, so she'd brought wine and chocolates.

"Hi, Steph!" Ellie's second son, Joseph, fumbled the screen door as he let her in, blushing furiously.

"Hey, Joseph. How did your basketball game go?"

His face fell. "We lost."

"Did you learn anything about what to do better?"

"Yeah. Maybe."

"Then you won, in the long run. I've learned more from my failures than my successes."

Joseph looked skeptical. "Seriously?"

She chuckled. "I know. Sounds like BS, right?"

"Kinda."

She bent and kissed his cheek. He turned bright pink. "You'll do better next time. I believe in you."

Too-earnest eyes stared into hers, and she flinched from the faith she saw there. What did she know about normal kids? She'd spent years trying to keep her mother from killing herself, only to fail in the worst way possible when she wasn't much older than Joseph.

Learn from your failures, indeed.

"Hi, Steph!" Ellie's eldest, Christy, approached and held out a hand. "You're supposed to take things from the guests, goofball," she said to her brother.

Joseph looked stricken. "Sorry."

"No need to be. We were having an important discussion, right?"

He had the sweetest smile. Some girl was going to be very lucky one day. "Right." He took the wine from her hands.

"Dad was asking for you," Christy told her brother.

"Okay." He started to turn, then looked back. "You're sitting by me at dinner, Steph."

"Fabulous. Nothing I love better than dining with a handsome man." She winked at him.

He blushed and stumbled over his feet as he turned, then hastened away.

"He has a crush on you. So does Davey."

"They have good taste."

Christy grinned.

"And who do you have a crush on, missy?"

Christy glanced away. "No one."

Huh. Was there a story here? "You okay?"

Her nod was too hasty. "I'm fine." She took the chocolates and moved away.

Steph wondered if she should delve further, but what did she know about parenting? Good parenting, that was. She knew far too much about the ways it could be done wrong.

Meanwhile, Ellie's daughter clearly welcomed a change of topic, so Steph obliged. "So where's the paragon?"

"Who?"

"The carpenter with a heart of gold. Mr. Perfect."

"Gavin." Christy giggled. "Back here." She drew Steph into the kitchen and toward a window overlooking the back porch.

"Glad you made it, Steph," Ellie said, smiling wide as she entered the room filled with amazing scents.

"Thank you for inviting me. What can I do to help?"

"We're fine here," Ellie said. "Gavin's outside."

Steph rolled her eyes.

Ellie's smile only became more beatific. Just then gorgeous music wafted through the open window, and her gaze was drawn toward it.

A man sat there, playing guitar and singing.

So. Gavin O'Neill.

She had to admit that the man had a beautiful baritone voice.

He wasn't half-bad looking, either, at least from his strong profile. Though seated, he was clearly an imposing man, built like a lumberjack. Steph leaned against the sill and watched his big hands finger the strings with surprising agility, notes of astonishing richness and depth emerging from the guitar, intertwining with his voice and the second Preston daughter Sarah's in a melody so haunting that all activity around the house had stopped.

Steph listened, soon caught up in the spell, and was astounded to feel her eyes fill. She couldn't remember the last time she'd cried, but not to respond to the pain and longing in this music would require a heart made of stone.

He looked up suddenly and caught her gaze.

She quickly looked away.

When the last notes died off, there was a long hush of respect for something extraordinary. Then from all quarters burst enthusiastic applause.

Gavin nodded and smiled, then his gaze returned to the window.

Steph retreated from view.

At that moment Ellie's youngest, Sam, skidded out on the porch. "Wow! Can you teach me to do that? Only not something so girly?"

Everyone broke up with laughter, including Gavin.

"Like this, you mean?" Gavin launched into a rousing tune filled with war and bloodshed and enough battles to thrill a little boy's urge for mayhem and set toes tapping.

Steph smiled as she moved to join Ellie.

"I told you he was amazing," her friend said. "He's restoring an old house, builds furniture like an artisan, gardens, cooks—"

"*So* not my type."

"Maybe your type needs changing."

"How about we talk about Laken's wedding instead?" Steph retorted.

"Coward. But okay." Ellie grinned. "Michael is chomping at the bit to tie her down before she finds a way to wiggle out of it."

"Will she?" Steph personally thought the verdict could go either way. Laken had seemed to concede, then gotten squirrelly again. Living with her must be exhausting.

"Not if she has a brain in her head. Michael is the best of men."

"And too good to be true," Steph said.

Ellie frowned. "No, he's just good. There's nothing wrong with that, is there? I hope you won't be saying that to Laken," she chided.

Awkward silence fell. Steph looked away, reminded of how much she didn't belong here. Only problem was, she didn't know where she did belong. If such a place existed.

"Steph, I'm sorry. That was wrong of me. I can't tell you

how to conduct your friendship." Ellie looked stricken.

"Surely there's something I can do to help." Steph wanted off that topic.

"One of the kids can get it."

"Ellie, please. Let me do something." *Or let me go. Away from all this smothering saccharine togetherness I thought I was escaping.*

"All right. Would you get me some ice from the utility porch?"

"On it." She quickly complied, glad to escape. Holidays gave her the willies at the best of times. Outside, she yanked on the stubborn latch of the ice chest and broke a nail down to the quick. She swore darkly and sucked on her finger.

"Is that any way for a lady to talk?"

Steph whirled around to see the paragon himself approaching. "I'm no lady. Anyway, you shouldn't sneak up on people."

"I didn't mean to scare you. Want some help?"

Of course his speaking voice would be as gorgeous as his singing one, the drawl slow and dark as molasses. "I'm doing fine, thank you." She dropped her injured finger to her side.

"No, you're not. Let me take a look at your hand." He stepped forward. "I'm Gavin O'Neill."

She stuck her hand behind her back. "I know who you are. Ellie's playing matchmaker, you do realize."

"Me? With you?" His eyes rounded.

"You don't have to sound so insulted. You're not my type, either, just so you know."

"Sure of that already?"

"You're not?"

"You're one to make snap judgments, are you?"

She shrugged. "Saves time."

He flashed a bright smile. "And clearly you'd like me to go away. Are you always so prickly or is it Ellie's intentions that have put the burr up your lovely behind?"

"It's my behind, and I'll thank you not to be watching it."

A lovely low rumble shook him. "I'm pretty sure any man with eyes couldn't possibly accommodate that demand. It's a very fine derrière, and I suspect you know that."

His blue eyes twinkled with amusement that only irritated her more. "Well then, why don't you lift this big ole ice chest for li'l ole me?" She batted her lashes. "Ellie needs more inside."

The corners of his eyes crinkled with his rumbling laughter, his cheeks denting with dimples. He leaned past her and picked up the chest as though it weighed nothing. "Why, of course, sugarplum," he answered in an exaggerated drawl. "Just tell this poor dumb redneck where you want it." The gleam in his eyes said he knew her game but he was too good-natured to mind.

He was definitely too nice for her. Not one iota her type. She liked edgy, dangerous men.

Though one of those had framed her and nearly killed her, not that long ago, she reminded herself.

She really needed out of here. She'd make it through the meal, then she was history.

But she had to sigh a little as her gaze roamed over the flexing of his muscular back and arms. Too bad she didn't dare take that very fine physique for a test drive.

Gavin surveyed the group numbering nearly thirty scattered over the huge dining table and assorted card tables strung into one long banquet. He rose from his seat, wine glass in hand. "To Ellie, who brings new meaning to the words domestic goddess."

"Hear, hear," replied Wyatt. "Best of all, *my* domestic goddess." He bent to his wife and gave her a lingering kiss. Ellie blushed, a secret smile on her lips.

"Get a room, you two. There are innocent children present," Steph teased from her place beside him.

The eldest Preston boy, fifteen-year-old Davy, stared at Steph adoringly. He and twelve-year-old Joseph seemed to think the woman was hot. Gavin couldn't disagree—if, that is, one had a self-destructive bent. She was a tall, curvy, bad-tempered siren, and if for a moment as she'd watched him sing, he'd seen a sadness in her eyes that had touched him, well—

He had more regard for himself, that fine derrière notwithstanding.

"They do that stuff all the time, Steph," Sam piped up. "We just ignore them."

The assembled group rang with laughter.

"What does your family do for Thanksgiving, Gavin?" asked Sarah.

"Pretty much what you do here: cook mountains of food and eat far too much of it." He leaned across the table, pitching his voice lower. "And don't you tell my mama because she's a great cook, but I've never had these foods prepared more deliciously than today."

Steph stirred. "I agree, but I have no idea why you put yourself through this, Ellie. You cook for three days, and in minutes, it's demolished. What's the point?"

"A woman's lot in life." Ellie shrugged. "I enjoy feeding people."

"Not this woman," Steph muttered.

Gavin glanced to see if Ellie had heard. "Must you?" he asked Steph, keeping his voice low.

"What?"

"Your cynicism is misplaced here."

"Who appointed you the etiquette police?" she whispered furiously.

They were beginning to draw attention. "We'll discuss this later."

"We won't speak at all, if I have any say." Steph turned to Joseph on her other side. The boy was clearly smitten with her.

The conversation and laughter continued unabated around them, but she said not one more word to Gavin as the meal wound down. He was inclined to be grateful. Her tone was as sharp as her attitude, and she was rude to boot.

She was surely wrong about Ellie's intent to match them up. Ellie wouldn't do such a thing to him. No one could be further from the woman of his dreams.

A few hours later, however, the woman was still on his mind as he returned home after a long day. He had risen early to work at the job he was close to finishing before going to the Preston home. There was trim to run, and he'd wanted the space and quiet to do it properly. There was a peace to be found in measuring and cutting, fitting pieces together in a joint so smooth and sweet that no one would be able to spot it easily.

He should be tired and ready for bed, but he wasn't. His thoughts kept returning to his prickly dinner companion, who hadn't hung around long after the meal. He didn't know why he should be sparing her one second's consideration.

Except that he couldn't seem to stop remembering his first sight of her as she watched him sing.

When she thought no one was watching, she'd had her heart in her eyes, a heart that had known pain, had suffered greatly. He'd almost have said the woman was lonely.

At the time, however, he hadn't been aware of how out of character such vulnerability would be, how difficult she actually was.

But then there was her behavior with the Preston children. Around them, everything about her softened. Her claws retracted and she could be almost...sweet.

He didn't know what her story was, but the contrasts made him want to dig deeper.

Blast his hide.

And here he'd said he had no self-destructive instincts. He shook his head as he unlocked the workshop he'd made from an old ramshackle garage behind his house. A warm, furry shape appeared beside him, the scarred head bumping the side of his knee.

"Good evening, my friend," Gavin greeted Finn, the half-blind border collie he'd found on another jobsite a few months back. He dug his fingers into the now-silky hair that had once been matted and full of burrs, his fingers kneading the old dog's neck and shoulders.

Finn groaned and leaned into him.

Gavin sank to his haunches and sent the dog into ecstasy, his tail thumping eagerly on the wood floor. At the commotion, another figure appeared in the doorway, Lily, the mama cat who'd once owned this space until he and she had made their peace with one another. She twined her way past Finn and rubbed against his leg. "How are you, darlin'?"

He gave both animals a good stroking—and then he laughed. *My Gavin, the savior of strays*, his mother called him. He had a radar for a lost cause, a sad case, she claimed. Perhaps so, but if he had one grain of sense in his thick skull, he'd ignore any such notions about Steph Hargrove.

Which, clearly, she wouldn't welcome anyway.

Gavin rose and walked to his workbench, studying the jewelry box that was his current project, wondering exactly who he was making it for. He didn't always know until he was finished, but the making of something new was a challenge, a puzzle to be solved.

He would spend an hour or so at the end of this long day focusing only on these pieces of wood that would become something beautiful, and he would cease to care if the lady was lonely.

He didn't need the headache.

You're not my type, she'd said. Nor was she remotely his own.

Resolutely Gavin put his hands to work, and after a bit, his mind followed, leaving sad-eyed women behind.

She'd lost her edge since leaving Seattle. It was time to revive the Steph who'd saved her, ditch this cautious, sad ghost who'd replaced the ballbuster siren. Trusting Ty Grant had nearly gotten her killed, and she had retreated into a shell. She'd even—heaven help her—flirted with the notion that the Sweetgrass way, that wholesome, *love-fixes-everything* world could be hers.

Thank heavens she'd returned to her senses, not a moment too soon.

The only time in her life she'd felt in control was when she was calling the shots. After a childhood when she'd been at the mercies of fate and a drug-addled mother, she'd made certain she was always in charge of her life. When she was the one who went after what she wanted. She was not and never would be a shrinking violet.

So Steph was getting back into the swing of life with a vengeance that very night. She hit a couple of clubs that were open even on Thanksgiving, had danced until her restless feet hurt. She'd flirted, been propositioned, had considered and dropped several candidates, but in the end, she'd returned to her loft alone, still trying to clear her mind of the aggravating carpenter.

There was only one major difference from her past this night: she'd come home alone.

Now she sat on her second-floor windowsill, one leg propped up, the other dangling over empty air. Looking down, she watched the entertainment district stragglers, wondering if any felt her watching their little dramas unfold. Across the street, a decrepit Ford van crawled away, carrying the house band to a wee-hours breakfast where they'd laugh and talk and divide the night's take among them.

Someone whistled back behind her, a tune so achy and sad she wanted to beg him to stop.

"Hey, gorgeous," a graveled voice called right below her.

Steph looked down.

Guitar strapped across his back, he was young…too young, but wise in the ways of the street, she could see that. Hard times rode the planes of his face, nestled in the long hair drifting over his shoulders. "Whatcha doin' up there, pretty lady?"

Steph smiled. "Not much. You?"

He shrugged. "Just gettin' by." He pantomimed strumming his guitar. "Playin' some tunes…takin' it as it comes." He smiled, slow and sweet. "Layin' down tracks for tomorrow."

Steph leaned her cheek against her knee, unwelcome but too-familiar emptiness echoing inside her. "That ol' tomorrow. She's not so easy to get to sometimes."

He chuckled. "You are so right, sweet one." He pulled his guitar around the front. "Maybe I can help you along."

Steph nodded, feeling a pinch in her heart at the kindness of a stranger.

He began strumming, then blended his smooth voice with words she couldn't make out.

It didn't matter. The melody spoke for itself. He played about love and longing…about pain and parting and nights when you don't think you'll make it until tomorrow.

He was good, but he made her remember Gavin O'Neill's voice, his hands on the strings. The kindness in his eyes she didn't want. Didn't need. The laughter that came to him so easily.

Except with her. He didn't approve of her.

Which was fine because she was not going to think about that man anymore. Ever.

Suddenly she itched to escape her thoughts, to leap inside and slam the window.

But at that moment, the man below switched to a melody so light, so hopeful that Steph's heart lifted, just a little.

Not much. But sometimes, even a little was enough.

She leaned her head back against the frame and closed her eyes, drifting inside the cradle his music had made for her. For moments that felt safely endless, she let him wrap a soft, cozy cocoon of music around her, and her heart rested.

Unlike the way Gavin's music had made her feel exposed.

Stop. Just…stop. Wearily, she tried to return to that place of rest, but…no dice.

When the last notes trailed off, Steph bent forward. "Come up."

He smiled and let his gaze slide over the length of her. "With legs like those, I won't say it's not tempting." Then he shook his head. "But that's not what you need, is it?"

Steph chewed at her lower lip, then sighed. Damn it, he was right. She shook her head. "I think I can sleep now. Thank you."

He slanted a lazy salute. "That's thanks enough for me." Turning to go, he looked back one more time. "Sleep tight, pretty lady." Then he shambled off.

With a lump in her throat, Steph climbed back inside her loft, closing the window behind her.

And went to be alone. Again.

Chapter Three

The country-western bar where Gavin let himself be dragged after work several days later was one favored by an odd mix of cowboys, construction workers and white-collar types who liked to kick back a few and dance. It reminded him of a honky-tonk he'd loved back home.

For some of the guys from Wyatt's jobsite, this was their usual after-work stop, and Gavin found himself not averse to indulging in a beer on this day.

Uncharacteristically, Wyatt had accompanied them. Gavin sat beside him at the bar, raised his glass of the brew to salute the man who'd become one of his closest friends. "What are you doing here? You usually head straight home."

Wyatt actually...squirmed? "I like doing that. You don't do this much, either, am I right?"

"I'm remodeling a house in my spare time, if you'll recall."

"You'd have an easier go of it if you leveled the place and started from scratch."

Gavin smiled. "But where would be the challenge in that?"

"You do seem to like a test." He hesitated.

"What's on your mind?" Because something clearly was.

Wyatt paused, then cleared his throat. "Look, just a friendly word of warning: stay away from Steph Hargrove. I saw you together at our place. She's bad news."

"What makes you say that?" Not that he disagreed.

"She has a troubled past—and a reputation that reminds me too much of Laken."

"Laken?"

"That's right—you've never met her. She's an old friend of Ellie's, but she lives in Sweetgrass Springs now."

"Where we'll be starting the new job soon," Gavin noted.

"That's right. The guy Steph works for, Jackson Gallagher, keeps buying up buildings there to make room for employees he's moved from Seattle. He's become a one-man economic development machine."

"Video games, right? *Doom Galaxy*?"

"Yeah. Great game, huh? My boys are crazy about it. Jackson said I could bring them with me one day. Let them beta-test the game they're finishing now."

"Really?"

"Want in on the action?" Wyatt asked.

"Absolutely."

Both fell silent. Finally, Wyatt cleared his throat again. "So. Steph."

"What about her?"

"I've spent several years watching Laken discard men like used tissues. Steph seems cut from the same mold. I have no idea why Ellie is so determined to adopt her, except Ellie can't resist a lost cause. Or a stray...sort of like you, come to think of it. This stray has a bite, though, I'd bet anything." Wyatt met his gaze. "And if you say one word to Ellie about this warning, I'm firing you, I don't care how talented you are."

"You can't." Gavin grinned. "Ellie likes me."

"She's matchmaking."

"I know. She means well."

"I told her not to."

"If it makes you feel any better, Ms. Hargrove isn't thrilled, either."

"How about you?"

"She's absolutely not my type."

"She's sexy as hell, though," Wyatt pointed out.

"She is that."

"If you only want a roll in the hay, I'm betting she's very talented."

Gavin frowned. "Your kids like her. And I have a feeling she might be lonely."

A bark of laughter. "Steph? I doubt that." Wyatt glanced in the mirror behind the bar, and his brow wrinkled. "Speak of the devil…she does get around, doesn't she?"

Gavin followed his stare and spotted the woman in question striding across to the bar on those long, long legs, her lithe figure showcased in a tight black pinstriped skirt and severely tailored red silk blouse. Work clothes, he supposed, but with the addition of red stilettos, she looked anything but buttoned-up.

She was quickly welcomed by the bartender and offered a stool by one of the regulars. She gave each man around her a smile that seemed genuine, bantering with them and making every man near her vie for her attention. Steph Hargrove was a siren, yes, but with a surprising dash of pal mixed in. In no time she had her audience eating from her hand.

"I'd better shove off." Wyatt signaled the bartender to bring his check. "I'll be late for Joseph's game if I don't get cracking."

Just then Steph glanced into the mirror, and her gaze fastened on Gavin's. He felt a visceral and very unwelcome punch, but he carefully kept his face neutral and merely lifted his beer in salute.

She arched one eyebrow, then pointedly turned away.

Friendly perhaps, but not to him. And didn't that just stir the competitor in him?

Wyatt rose and clapped his hand on Gavin's shoulder. "Look, you're a grown man. I should butt out."

Gavin grinned. "You should. But I'm doubting you will."

Wyatt chuckled. "Probably true." Then he followed Gavin's gaze and frowned. "Your funeral. Just don't say I didn't warn you."

Gavin touched his forehead in salute. "Forewarned is forearmed."

"You'd need some serious armor with that one. Well, see you." He turned away, then back. "Oh—I'm supposed to find out if you'll be around for Christmas."

"That's family time," Gavin responded.

"Are you going home to Tennessee?"

"No, not this year. One of my sisters is having a baby in January, so I'll see them then."

"Then come be with us. As you might have noticed, Ellie has a generous definition of family. You won't be the only non-Preston in attendance, I assure you." He frowned. "But Steph might be there."

"She doesn't have family?"

"Don't know. Haven't heard any mentioned." Wyatt clapped him on the back. "See you in the morning."

Gavin nodded absently. There might be the explanation for Stephanie's behavior—yes, Stephanie. Steph was too harsh a name, to his ears. Not that he expected to be calling her anything, really.

He should head out, as well. There was sheetrock calling his name.

But just then he noticed her on the small dance floor, smiling and flirting outrageously with her current partner.

Gavin pondered holding sheetrock...or holding her.

No question she'd caught his attention, like it or not. She was an itch that would keep niggling at him until he figured out how to scratch it. Surely one more encounter with her would cure him of this curious fascination, since they were so clearly unsuited. He threw some money down on the bar, and headed her direction.

As he approached, she glanced over her shoulder, then

quickly turned her back on him, redoubling her attention on her partner, putting a dangerous sway in those slim hips he wouldn't mind getting his hands on.

She's bad news.

Hadn't he had his own taste of her sharp tongue? Indeed, but abruptly Gavin found himself smiling. She was bad-tempered and difficult, but didn't that add to the challenge she presented? His perfect woman hadn't yet made her appearance, and while he was patiently waiting, he would unlock the puzzle of Stephanie Hargrove. It wasn't as though his heart would get involved, after all. His heart wasn't what heard her siren call. And he wasn't a monk.

Meanwhile, two could play Ms. Hargrove's game.

When Stephanie glanced over and narrowed her eyes at him as if to warn him off, he stifled the grin that threatened and instead walked right past her toward a woman sitting with her friends. This woman was definitely more his type with her generous curves and sweet face. "Would you care to dance?"

"Me? I, uh…" She glanced at her friends.

"Only the one dance. I swear my mom would tell you I'm just a hair stubborn but, on the whole, quite harmless."

"You're not from here," said one of her friends.

The first woman smiled. "I love your accent. Where in the South?"

"East Tennessee, but you're the one with the music in her voice."

Her friend grinned. "If you don't want him, Sue Anne, I do."

He smiled right back. "Perhaps you two ladies would also favor me with a dance."

"I'm taken," said one.

"I'm not," said the second.

"Get in line," said Sue Anne.

Gavin laughed and drew her out on the dance floor where they chatted easily. He never once spared a glance for

Stephanie.

At the end of that song, he escorted Sue Anne back and claimed her friend. The third woman said her boyfriend was out of town, so she wanted her turn, too.

"Oh, but I would never go after another man's woman. My mama would tan my backside."

"Drat," sighed the woman. "A gentleman."

This time Gavin had a more difficult time ignoring Stephanie completely because she somehow wound up right next to them. When he glanced her way, she gave him her best come-hither look, then redoubled her efforts to charm her current dance partner, her movements sinuous and seductive. When the man's hands slid around to grab the derrière Gavin had admired, Gavin had to contain a glower.

"Uh-oh," said his partner. "Lovers' quarrel?"

"Not at all."

"She keeps watching you, you know, when you're not looking."

Gavin stifled a satisfied smile. "You don't say."

"Want me to go tell her she's stupid for doing whatever it is that has you dancing with us instead of her?"

Gavin laughed heartily and was pleased to see Stephanie's head whip in his direction. "A friend of mine calls her a man-eater."

The woman glanced over. "She looks like one. Sue Anne's much nicer."

"I'm sure. And much more my type." Gavin sighed. "But there's that stubborn part my mama would warn you about. I'll play this hand out."

"My advice? Get Sue Anne's phone number first."

Gavin chuckled. "Perhaps I will." The music stopped, and he escorted her back to their table, pausing long enough to visit for a few minutes, leaving with not one but two phone numbers even after Sue Anne's friend told Sue Anne the score.

Gavin left them, debating simply leaving now.

The band began again, a slow, smoky tune, and he reversed course, snagging Stephanie from her current companion. "My turn."

The man protested, but Gavin's expression stopped him. He shrugged and moved off.

She jerked in his grasp. "I didn't say I wanted to dance with you."

"Hush." He drew her into him and began moving.

She remained stiff. "What, you want to give me another lecture?"

He merely held her more snugly against him. "Sh-h. I like this song."

He saw the mutiny in her eyes along with the confusion. Bit by bit, though, she relented, and he smiled to himself, tucking her head into his shoulder and swinging them around so that she had no choice but to hang onto him.

Soon she quit resisting completely, then swiveled her hips against him in a blatant invitation Gavin badly—*badly*—wanted to pursue.

Instead, he whirled them again.

And began to sing to her.

Stephanie lifted her head, a line forming between her eyebrows, and he could see her working up an argument.

But to his amazement, she subsided and simply danced, their bodies surprisingly attuned to each other. Once in a while, she'd look at him, baffled.

But she didn't move away.

They danced that dance and two more before the band took a break, exchanging not one word the entire time.

As their bodies separated, Gavin could see her gearing up again to seduce him, to make him simply one of the many, so he seized the initiative to keep her off balance. "Evenin', Miz Stephanie. I'll see you soon." He kissed her knuckles when he wanted to kiss her beautiful mouth. "Need a ride home first?"

Her lips parted, her eyes first confused, then anger reappeared. "Of course not. Anyway, the night's barely begun." She studied his reaction with a sideways glance. "And my name is Steph."

"It doesn't suit you. I've decided I like Stephanie better."

Her brows snapped together. "Excuse me?"

I do believe I have your number, Ms. Hargrove. "Tomorrow's a work day," he said blithely. "You'll need your sleep."

"Bed, perhaps," she all but purred. "I don't need much sleep."

He clamped down as every instinct he possessed prodded him to drag her out of here, to seize what she so blatantly offered.

But that would make him forgettable like all the others. Why that mattered, he wasn't sure. He only knew he wasn't done with her yet.

Oh, no, sweetheart. We'll play this my way. "Sweet dreams to you, then." He turned to go.

"Good night and good riddance." Vexation filled her tone.

Gavin didn't let himself turn back.

But he left with a smile on his face.

Chapter Four

She wanted to sit on her windowsill, damn it. Steph stared in frustration at the cold drizzle that had set in before she arrived home from work the next night. She needed to think, needed more space to prowl. The walls of her loft were closing in. The weather was nasty, but she had to get out of here, away from the silence. Music didn't get it; TV was worse. She'd picked up two different books and tossed both of them in disgust.

Making up her mind quickly, she strode toward her coat rack. A sharp crack against her window drew her up short.

What the—?

There it was again. Pea gravel. Sharp little clicks against her window.

Why didn't whoever it was just use the buzzer?

When the third shower of stones clinked, Steph strode across the floor in a huff, jerking the window open.

She leaned out. "Why don't you use the stupid buzz—?" The words dried up in her throat at the sight of the man on the sidewalk.

Gavin O'Neill.

Under the hood of his coat, his face creased in a smile. "If you won't answer the phone when I call, why should I expect you to answer the buzzer?"

He'd walked out on her the night before, when she wasn't

through with him. And yes, thanks to Caller ID, she'd ignored a phone call earlier. "So you threw rocks at my window?"

"Ah, but gently, darlin', with exactly the right touch. Same as how I treat a woman, you see."

"You probably think that." She shrugged indifferently. "Men often overrate their performance." Now he'd be insulted and go away.

But of course he didn't do that. Instead, he threw back his head and laughed, that deep, rolling sound that reached right past every barrier she could put up.

"Does that work with your usual victim? If so, you definitely haven't met the right man yet."

"Are you asking to be one of them? I'll warn you I don't keep anyone around long."

His eyes widened in mock horror. "They allow you to send them away?"

"I prefer to sleep alone."

"Well, then, darlin' Stephanie, you clearly haven't slept with the right man."

"You think you're him?" Her tone dripped condescension.

"Don't be getting ahead of yourself. I haven't even decided if I like you yet." His smile was unrepentant.

She had to grin back. His unfailing good humor made it difficult to stay mad at him. "You are unbelievably annoying, Gavin O'Neill. I can't decide if you're dumb as a post or the most arrogant man I've ever met."

"While you're pondering, I'll be right up. Hit the lock."

"Wait—I didn't say you—"

Too late. He'd already disappeared from sight.

Steph slammed down the sticky window, shivering from the cold air that had filled the room. She should just leave him out there in the rain. It was so bone-deep cold that he'd soon leave.

But until he did, she was trapped in here, the same cage

she'd been clawing to escape.

Damn the man. Abruptly Steph laughed out loud. What the hell—she'd been wanting entertainment, but she'd never in a million years imagined it being Gavin. She crossed the floor and punched the button, wondering just when she'd lost control of the situation.

Probably about five seconds after they'd met.

But she'd get it back, and then she'd boot him out, just like the others.

He didn't knock but instead turned the knob and walked right in, standing in the doorway dripping. "That's my girl. I knew you wouldn't leave a man to freeze."

Steph nodded toward the coat rack on the wall. "Hang up your coat right there."

He did so, even going so far as to pull off his boots, but his eyes were busy taking in the space around him. She had a sense of all her secrets being bared.

Gavin took his sweet time, not moving from where he stood, barely less imposing in his socks. He glanced up, and his face wreathed in smiles. "Pressed tin ceiling, bless my soul." Glancing back at her, he shook his head. "An interesting jumble. Secrets here to be mined, darlin' Stephanie. A man could spend some time doing it."

"Don't get any ideas. I only took pity on a fool who'd stand out in the rain."

"That you did, sweetheart, and there'll be stars in your crown for it." He rubbed his hands together. "You wouldn't happen to have a beer, would you?"

Steph snorted. "Do I look like a beer girl?"

Blue eyes twinkled. "Maybe you haven't had a beer with the right man. You may not yet be up to the challenge of a man like me, but I just might be willing to take on the task of grooming you for it."

"You wish." She shrugged nonchalantly. "I've probably got some tequila and limes. We could try body shots."

"I might be persuaded to try."

She had to chuckle. "You're telling me you've never done body shots before?" She walked toward the kitchen area, all too aware of his large frame right behind her. As a tall woman, she wasn't used to feeling dainty, but that's exactly how he made her feel.

"I've never done them with you, sugar."

She felt the zing in her blood but worked hard to ignore it. "Yeah, yeah, yeah. Here we go. You can have..." But he'd left her, his concentration already switched to something else.

Her kitchen faucet? She'd never had a man up to her place who'd paid more attention to her apartment than her body. Right now, he was turning handles, then using those capable hands to unscrew something on the tip of the faucet.

He shook the metal piece and slapped it against his palm until a tiny screen fell into his hand. Gavin held it up to the light, frowning. "This screen needs replacing. And how long has this faucet been dripping?"

"I just moved in. Anyway, what business is it of yours?"

He glanced around. "I suppose it's too much to expect that you'd have a toolbox?"

"Of course I do. No twenty-first century woman is without one," she huffed.

"Lead the way, sweetheart."

Steph grabbed for the part. "Give me that. I can take care of my own repairs, thank you very much."

Placing the metal whatever-it-was and screen in her hand, he executed a sweeping invitation. "Please. I love to watch a woman work."

"I'll do it later." She slapped the parts on the counter and turned away.

"Oh, but there's no time like the present, didn't anyone teach you that?" Gavin relaxed against the counter, arms crossed, a big smile on his face. "Humor me. I'm in no hurry."

"I'm not in the mood." Steph walked past him, drinks

forgotten.

His arm shot out and wrapped around her waist, pulling her close. "Damn, but I do enjoy the way you do that."

She leaned back, all too aware of how well they fit together. "Do what?"

His other hand slid up her back, tunneling into her hair, tilting her head slightly. "Lie with such arrogance." His head lowered to hers, and he growled softly.

Then it was too late. His mouth covered hers, his big body surrounding her. She could smell wood shavings on him, pine and cedar and soap…and something else she could only describe as all man.

Faster than she would ever have believed, his kiss swept her mind clean of any thought but him. For one perilous, treacherous moment, she remembered how it felt to dance with him, to have her body tight against his muscled one. A part of her wanted nothing more than to snuggle up in those strong arms, to sink into the comfort of him.

No. Oh, no. But before she could end the kiss, he did, then set her back on her feet. She stifled a moan.

Regret shone in those blue eyes, and he trailed one finger down her cheek. "There won't be any more of that until we get something straight between us."

Steph bristled and stepped away, fixing him with a baleful stare. "And just what might that be?"

"When you're ready to tell all those boys you play with that you're finished with them."

"And why on earth would I do that?"

"Because you're gonna be spending your time with me now, Stephanie darlin'. And I don't share."

She laughed, though it wasn't as steady as she'd have liked. "You can't be serious."

He tapped his chest. "Don't be listening to your head now. It's the heart that's speaking to you."

"You're insane. I told you you're not my type. Anyway,

I'm still mad at you for dressing me down at Thanksgiving."

He shrugged. "You know I was right. A family like that needs supporting, not being sneered at."

"I wasn't sneering. I think they're great."

"But?"

She turned away. "They're an anomaly. Marriage isn't like that."

"Your parents?" His gaze warmed with sympathy.

"My parents are none of your business."

"What if I'm making you my business?"

"Don't bother. I'm not interested."

"Liar." He approached her again.

She backed away. "We couldn't be more different. I'm a shark business exec. I'm very good at what I do. You're a—"

"Careful now. Wouldn't want to let your high-and-mighty streak show too much. I'm a simple carpenter and not ashamed of it."

"I didn't say you should be. I'm not a snob."

Pity darkened his eyes. "Oh, but I think you are. Worse, I scare you. I see who you are, beyond the seductress, beyond the woman who pretends to be a man-eater."

Then, to her great surprise, he reversed course and headed for the door, pulling on his boots and sliding his arms into his coat. "I'm not afraid of you, Stephanie. You won't discard me like the others. I'll go when I'm ready and not a minute before."

"First I'd have to get involved, and that's not gonna happen."

"It will. Get ready for it."

"It won't." But she wrapped her arms around her waist against a sudden shiver.

"I don't say it will be easy—God knows you're anything but that. I've surely lost my mind getting involved with you, but too late now." He grasped the door handle, then turned back, giving her a long, soulful look she couldn't interpret.

"I'm not what you think you want, sweetheart, but I'm exactly what you need."

Then he smiled and gave a tiny salute. "It's a good thing I'm a patient man, Stephanie darlin'. I have a feeling I'm going to need every speck of it I can muster." He glanced toward the kitchen. "Just screw the end back on like it was. It will do overnight. I'll be back with the tools and parts tomorrow."

Without another word, he was out the door.

Steph raced after him, grasping the handle with a thought to call him back, to demonstrate her disdain and leave him in no doubt of who had the upper hand.

Instead she let go and leaned back heavily against the wood. She swore, but her heart wasn't really in it. Drawing herself up resolutely, she headed to the kitchen to put her faucet back together and resume the life she liked just fine.

You have a high opinion of yourself, Gavin O'Neill.

Insane. The man was certifiable.

And definitely not her type.

But even though her sample was brief, she knew one sure thing about him.

The man could kiss. Suddenly Steph laughed out loud.

Certifiable, for sure. Not her type, definitely.

But able to make her toes curl?

Damn the man, yes.

Not that she'd ever tell him.

"You. Off the equipment. Now."

Laken jolted at the voice barking orders over the volume of her iPod. Jeanette Roundtree stood there in all her bossy glory.

Laken pulled out one earbud but kept the treadmill in Enigma's fitness center going. "What?"

"Chop-chop. I don't have all day. Off the treadmill."

"Excuse me?"

But Jeanette refused to continue until Laken did as she'd asked—ordered, really. Though she was no longer working at Ruby's except when there was special need, Jeanette was too accustomed to telling the waitresses what to do. Customers, too, come to think of it.

They'd become sort-of friends, though they butted heads as often as not. "You're not the boss of me." She strolled over slowly, then stopped, hands on hips.

Jeanette ignored her defiance. "Drop the t-shirt. You're barely showing but you've sure got pregnancy boobs, don't you?" Jeanette grinned and patted her own. "Are they not the best? Walker can't get enough of them."

Laken stuck fingers in her ears. "La-la-la-la I can't hear you."

"You're just jealous because you're not really showing yet, but check this out." The tall blonde pulled her dress tight around her middle. "I am—isn't it great?"

Her bump barely showed. "You're a sick woman, Jeanette."

The other woman beamed. "Nope. Just happy. So happy. I never dreamed…" Then actual tears from the least sentimental person Laken knew filled her eyes, and Laken didn't have the heart to be snippy.

"I know you are, and I'm really glad for you. Walker's pretty amazing. You hit the jackpot with that one."

"I really did." Jeanette sniffed and wiped her eyes. "But your man ain't chopped liver, girlfriend. And he's clearly crazy about you."

"Yeah. I don't know why."

Jeanette chuckled. "Me either. You're such a pain the ass. So I just have one question for you."

Warily Laken nodded. "And that would be—"

"What the devil is wrong with you? You think men like Michael just grow on trees?"

"Around here they seem to." She didn't know why she was arguing.

"Okay, here's the deal: I don't have all day to stand around jawing with you when I only have three weeks to get your gown done."

"My...gown?" Then her earlier words hit. "Three...weeks?" she squeaked. "What's happening in—"

"You don't want to find yourself at the altar in a gown you had no say over, the way Scarlett and Ruby did? I did an awesome job on both, and I can do it again, but here's your chance: get on board before the train runs over you."

"I'm not getting married at—Christmas is only—" she spluttered. "Nobody's giving me a surprise wedding."

"They're not yet because I gave you fair warning." Jeanette pulled the tape measure from around her neck. "Now drop the t-shirt and get over here. You can still wear something form-fitting if you want to—heaven knows you exercise enough that everything is firm, and with the baby boobs—"

Laken went cold all the way through. "Does Michael know about this?" Surely he wouldn't spring something like this on her.

"No. Because there isn't a wedding planned yet, but Ruby has that look in her eyes, and Maddie and Scarlett have been on the phone a lot lately, talking where nobody can hear them. Brenda asked me if I thought you'd prefer roses or something more unique—you know she can make you an amazing bouquet. And Spike has sketched up some designs for a cake that are completely awesome, but—are you listening to me, girlfriend? You can have a say if you'll stop sticking your head in the sand. Everyone who cares about you will be here for the community Christmas, so you wouldn't be asking people to pull together a second special occasion. You and Michael can do this together and do it your way if you'll just get that stubborn head out of your—"

Laken tuned out, reeling. Three weeks? How could she possibly get married in three weeks? "It's too soon. There's not time to—"

"Laken." Jeanette was tapping her toe. "How old do you want that child to be when you finally make him legal? There is an end date on the process, you know that, right? So when were you going to get around to this? How much longer do you need to keep that good man waiting?"

"But—" Laken had to sit down. "I just—" She lifted terrified eyes to Jeanette. "What if we can't make it work?"

"You're already living together. You have been for close to two years now. What exactly do you think you still have to figure out?"

"I...don't know, but—"

"You love him, because you're not stupid. And he's crazy about you. Have you discovered some horrible habit he has that you can't tolerate? Does he leave the seat up or snore too loud or pick his nose or—"

Laken had to laugh. "No. Though he does have this habit of putting peanut butter on both pieces of bread before he puts on the jam."

"Well, thank God you'll be saved a lifetime of hell. Run away now. It's clear the man is a monster."

"Screw you." Laken looked at the floor, raking fingers through the hair that used to be so short but was at one of those awful in-between stages. "My hair. It's a wreck."

"Pretty sure that's fixable," Jeanette said drily. "What else you got?"

"Three...weeks. You can't make a dress in three weeks."

"Well, I can't if I don't get your measurements. So let's see: scary peanut butter habits, bad hair—" Jeanette was ticking off items on her fingers. "No dress." Then she met Laken's gaze head on. "No guts. And absolutely not a lick of sense. Anything else too horrible to contemplate?"

"It's not funny," Laken whispered.

Jeanette sat down beside her. "It's not. I know you're scared. What's the worst that could happen?"

Laken tensed. "My parents once thought they loved each

other, but it didn't last. They made my life hell—still would, if I'd let them."

"And all these happy couples in Sweetgrass never fight. Never get mad. Never say stupid things to each other. Do you know I told Walker just this morning that he was a moron because he let Maisie con him into another dog?"

Laken smiled. "Divorce court, definitely."

"Jackson and Veronica had to wait nearly twenty years to be together. Ian nearly lost Scarlett forever in childbirth. Gordon and Sophia did split up. There are no guarantees, Laken. Love doesn't come with a money-back guarantee. You have to work at it, every single day. Michael isn't worth some work?"

"Of course he is. But he doesn't need any work. He's perfect."

"Peanut butter," Jeanette reminded her.

"Per-fect," Laken enunciated. "But I'm not. I'm hard to live with."

"Yeah, poor Ajax looks so unhappy. And Michael hardly ever smiles. You are such a witch. You should leave town immediately."

"I can't—" Laken's voice caught, and she rested one hand on her still-flat belly. "There's a baby now. Who deserves everything good."

"Is it that you don't want to be a mother?"

Laken's head whipped around. "I want to be the best mother in the universe—" Her eyes filled. "But what if I can't?"

"You'll screw up sometimes," Jeanette said. "Do you think Scarlett has never raised her voice to Georgia? Or yelled at Ian? You think Bridger doesn't want to throw Penny off a bridge sometimes because she's so hardheaded? And I know you've seen Rissa yell at Mackey. But you know what they do? They work it. Every day. Some days they get mad or tired or worried, and everything's not all sunshine and roses. But they get up every day and go at it again, trying their best but being human." Her voice softened. "Has it ever occurred to you that you might be a really good mom precisely because you know what not to do? That you and Michael might still have tough times, but that you're not a wimp and neither is he, so you don't give up?" She paused. "Think about what life was like before Michael. Was it better? Richer? More fun?"

"No. It was—I was—"

"Lonely?"

She glanced over. "Were you?"

"You better believe it. I thought my life would always be waitressing at the café and watching other people live the life I wanted. I sure never expected Walker—or Maisie. I...sometimes I still get scared."

"Why?"

"Because love is terrifying. Because it's scary to care this much. Need this much. Anything could happen." Jeanette bit her lip.

"So what do you do?"

"Some days I get crazy, worrying. But then I see Walker pass through a room, and I can't breathe for what he makes me feel. So I try very hard to focus on that moment, that day. I watch Maisie play with her puppy and listen to Walker miss chords and cuss while he's composing a new song. I hear his voice singing, and I look around my tiny house that's bursting at the seams and I get so scared of losing it all that I'm about ten seconds from freezing, but—the love. It draws me away from the fear. It's this great big warm blanket that wraps around me and it's big enough to wrap around this family I love so much, so I hug Maisie and I kiss Walker and sit in his lap and I try really, really hard to believe that nothing bad will happen, but—"

"Sometimes it does."

"Sometimes it does. But you don't quit. Because if you do, what was the point of your miracle? If all this love is right there waiting for you to accept it, what kind of idiot would give it up and run away?" Jeanette met her gaze squarely.

"You're not a quitter, Laken, and you're not a total idiot."

"Gee, thanks."

"You're being an idiot right now, but that's not who you really are. You're too hardheaded to be such a coward. Jump over those doubts. Kick the crap out of that mound of worry and scatter it in every direction. You can embrace the fear or you can embrace the love and the joy. You can kiss the socks off that man, and you can press your palm against the belly that contains physical evidence of the love that man has brought into your life." She paused. "Yeah, you could give up and run away. But you can't stop time. And you can't expect that wonderful man to live in limbo forever. That's cruel. Michael doesn't deserve cruelty, does he?"

"Am I? Cruel to him?" The idea made her chest hurt.

"Holding him at arm's length all the time for fear something bad will happen? It will happen, Laken, if you keep giving this love half-measures. I don't really think half-measures is your style. And no, you can be bitchy, but I don't believe you have a cruel heart."

Laken stared off into the distance and thought about all the times Michael had smiled at her so openly, had held his arms wide, had been so ready to embrace her and all her insanities.

"I don't know why he loves me. If I could just understand why. It doesn't make sense."

"Love doesn't care about logic. Love just is. It's a gift to the receiver and the giver both. Could you stop loving Michael if you wanted to?"

Laken felt a huge dark pit open, and she hastily backed away from the mere thought of life without Michael's smiles, his off-key whistling, his easy manner, his tender and thrilling touch.

Then she remembered the shadows in his eyes when she would hesitate, when she gave only part of herself—

Just as her parents had done. All her life she'd felt starved for their love. Needed them so badly.

Michael needed his love returned. And she was slowly starving him. "Oh. My. God." She pressed fingers to her forehead, horror sweeping over her. "I've been doing to him what my parents did to me." She turned to Jeanette. "All the times he's only wanted me to love him back the way he—" She closed her eyes. "And he hasn't given up on me yet. He hasn't left. Not even when I'm withholding myself from him. Oh, Jeanette—I have to go find him. I have to tell him—" She jumped up and raced to the door.

There she halted. "Can I come by later and let you measure me? I promise I won't be long—"

Jeanette smiled. "Tomorrow is soon enough. You go be with Michael."

"Thank you." She heaved a breath of gratitude. "Seriously, thank you, Jeanette. I just...I didn't see this. How'd you get so wise?"

"I've always been wise. Just some people don't listen. And Laken—"

"Yeah?" Laken jittered with impatience.

"I won't say anything to anyone yet, but tomorrow—we'd best get this show on the road."

Laken's stomach flipped but this time it was excitement bubbling through her. "A Christmas wedding. In three weeks." She shook her head. "We're gonna need help. Because he won't want to elope, will he? He'll want the whole kit and caboodle." She felt her face stretching in a smile that felt the best she'd felt in...forever. "He's a romantic."

"He is. A good kind of man to have, don't you think?"

"Oh, yeah." Laken closed her eyes and wished she could just wink herself to his side. "I gotta go."

"Take off. You'll have the help you need. There's a whole town just itching to get started."

A whole town. A home. Her home, hers and Michael's.

Laken started laughing. "This is the craziest place—" Then she was off like a shot.

Jeanette was laughing as she left.

Chapter Five

Gavin found himself whistling as he traveled nearly-deserted downtown streets at eight o'clock on Saturday morning. He'd seen her puzzlement, felt her body respond to his. She wanted to fight what she felt, but she was attracted, he was certain.

Not that she would like it one bit, of course. Ms. Stephanie Hargrove was far too accustomed to ordering men about, to calling the shots. One glimpse of those stunning legs, and a man could go blind simply from that. She used her sexuality as a weapon, as a barrier to protect a heart he was ever more certain needed care.

Not that she was The One, of course. No, his ideal woman was still out there somewhere, and he would keep looking.

But in the meantime, he could help her, this hard-edged woman who had likely never cared for a houseplant, much less gardened. She probably lived on take-out. As for baking bread...the mere image of Stephanie Hargrove with flour dusting her apron and her hands buried in dough...

That made him laugh out loud.

He was quite clearly insane, of course, for getting involved. Between his inability to resist a challenge and his weakness for strays, he was, as his mama often told him, a lost cause.

But Stephanie most definitely needed someone to be kind

to her, to teach her that her cynicism was misplaced. That there were men with whom she could be real, men she could trust.

He wouldn't let himself go too far, however. To get caught up in a woman like her would be insanity, pure and simple. He might be soft in the head, but he wasn't an idiot. Yes, he felt more alive around her, on the edge of his seat to see what on God's green earth she would do next. She was few things he wanted and many he did not.

But she was damn sure never boring.

He chuckled again as he parked his truck in the deserted entertainment district, unloaded not only his tools but a sack of groceries. He'd been up for hours, but he'd bet his granny's soul Stephanie was still sleeping, so he'd come prepared not only to fix her faucet but to feed her as well.

He pressed her buzzer once, then again with no answer. He set down his toolbox, already peering around him for pebbles to toss at her window again.

"Oh, hell, it's you," came the irritated voice from the speaker. "Do you know what time it is?"

Gavin grinned. "Buzz me up, sugar. I come bearing breakfast."

"I don't eat breakfast," she muttered.

But she hit the button.

Steph unlocked the door, then sank back into the nearest chair and curled up, already back half-asleep.

Gavin strode through it seconds later, whistling.

She muttered and refused to open her eyes. "Go away."

"Now, darlin'…"

She could feel, actually *feel* the insufferable man grinning at her. She picked up the pillow beside her and covered her face with it. "I can't believe you have the nerve to show up at, what, dawn?"

"It's hardly dawn. I've been up for hours."

She threw the pillow in the direction of his voice.

Something heavy rattled, then thumped on the floor. Footsteps sounded, along with something being set on her counter. She curled in more tightly on herself and wished just then that she'd thought to grab a blanket. It was freaking cold, and she only wore a camisole and boxers.

More footsteps, then a blanket settled over her. He even tucked it in around her legs, then pressed a kiss to her hair. "Sweet dreams," he murmured.

Then the blasted man started humming.

Steph dragged the blanket over her head and tried to shut him out, but how on earth did you ignore a very large man clomping around your apartment, even if the tune he was singing was quite lovely?

Then the coffee grinder kicked in.

"I hate you," she shouted.

"Hm? Did you say something?"

I'm going to kill him. Dead. Worse than dead. As Steph plotted the ways she could make Gavin die a slow, painful death, he blithely continued humming and clomping, pausing to chuckle now and again...

Then she smelled the coffee.

And whimpered.

Another chuckle.

Steph was torn between plotting...and pleading.

Coffee won. "Please..." She stuck one arm out from beneath the blanket.

"In a bit. Anything good is worth the waiting. Not good to rush things."

"Gimme."

She heard him approach. Then...nothing.

Her eyelids fluttered. The suspense was killing her.

"Well?"

The blanket was peeled back. Gavin sank to his haunches, blue eyes alight with humor and a trace of pity. "Not a morning person, are you?"

"Coffee. I'm begging."

His smile widened. "And what would be the magic word?"

"I said please already."

"So you did." He swooped in for a quick kiss on her nose. Then he proffered a mug that smelled absolutely heavenly, holding it still out of reach. "Would this be what you're whimpering about?"

"I don't whimper." Much.

"Oh, darlin', I beg to differ. Now what, a man has to wonder, would a creature in such dire straits be willing to give in exchange?"

"It's too early for sex."

A quick flash of very white teeth. "Oh my…you certainly are out of sorts, aren't you? It's never too early for sex—but that wasn't what I meant."

"You're going to make me beg."

"Not exactly…beg…"

"I did say I hate you, right?"

"That you did. But I know it's simply that you're out of sorts like a cranky child."

And all the while, the delectable scent of that coffee was wafting into her nostrils.

"You don't really mean you hate me."

"I might."

"No, you don't. And lucky for you, my price is quite simple and easily met. A simple *Good Morning, Gavin*, that's it."

"Good morning, Gavin," she droned.

"Did I mention that a little enthusiasm would help?"

"You're annoyingly chipper in the mornings, aren't you?"

He grinned unrepentantly. "That I am."

"Good thing we're never having sex. I'd have to boot you out during the night or kill you at dawn."

"That, sugar buns, is another discussion altogether. I've made my conditions clear." His smile was cocky and completely unruffled as he cupped one hand behind his ear. "Now I don't believe I heard you properly the first time."

"Good morning, Gavin," she said through gritted teeth.

Then she threw off the blanket and uncurled herself. "Good morning, Gavin." Her voice rose as she did, and he stood, too. She walked right up to where her feet touched his boots. "Good morning, Gavin," she shouted, her teeth bared in a grimace.

He smiled. "Could still use some work to convince me of your sincerity, but I'm a merciful man."

She snatched the mug and growled, then walked around him toward her bathroom.

Once inside, she slammed the door, took a healthy swallow and leaned back against the wood as her taste buds danced over the best cup of coffee she'd had in…ever.

Steph slowly slid down the door, settled on the floor and indulged herself.

"You all right in there?" Gavin asked from the other side.

"Go away. I'm having a religious experience," she answered. She sipped again and closed her eyes in ecstasy.

On the other side of the wood, Gavin grinned.

And tried not to think about how she looked in those skimpy pajamas.

"Take your time, darlin'."

Steph smiled into her cup. "I intend to."

"Hey, man, how's it going?" Bridger Calhoun greeted Michael.

"Fine," answered Michael in a flatter tone than normal.

He was packing up his vet bag after checking over one of the horses.

Bridger's brows rose. "Trouble in paradise? Congrats on the baby, by the way. I just heard."

"Thanks. I imagine we'll be coming to see you in your professional capacity sometime soon."

"I hope not. I've done my share of emergency deliveries, but that will make an old man of you." Bridger grinned, lifting his son JJ out of the backpack carrier. "The little dude is making me old before my time already." His grin said the opposite, however.

"He's looking healthy. How's it going, JJ? Give me five?"

The black-haired one-year-old with his dad's amber eyes gave Michael a toothy grin. "Five!" he crowed. His little palm met Michael's.

"Good man!" Michael wondered if they'd have a boy or a girl, though he didn't care. As long as the baby was healthy and Laken made it through the delivery fine, he'd have it all.

"What's up?" Bridger asked. "Laken feeling okay so far?"

"Besides spending most evenings throwing up her toenails? She seems okay."

"How are the wedding plans coming along?"

"What wedding plans?" He had gotten his hopes up when she'd said yes, but lately...

"Oh." Bridger shook his head. "Man, I feel for you. Been there. Got the t-shirt. It sucks. But you have an edge—you got your woman knocked up."

"Don't let her hear you say that."

"I thought she'd decided to get married."

"Me, too. Then she started crab-walking sideways." Michael looked at the ground. "If I'd hauled her off to the JP the second she said yes, we'd be set, but stupid me, I wanted to marry her in front of the whole world. We have so many friends here and family, and I wanted them to be part of it, but—"

"You could get Maddie to do a surprise wedding for you

like she did for Scarlett and Ruby."

"Yeah, that would go over big. Laken would run in the other direction so fast my head would spin." Michael heaved a sigh. "I don't know what else I can do. I've tried to have faith enough for both of us, but..." He looked up. "How'd you convince Penny?"

"Caught her at a weak moment after she helped me deliver Maddie's fourth unexpectedly. Don't think you can count on that angle. Unless Laken goes gooey over puppies or colts or something."

"Yeah, not quite the same," Michael mourned.

"But I do have some good news to share."

"What? And if you tell me Penny's pregnant again, I don't want to hear it."

"Not yet," Bridger grinned. "We're back to practicing for a while, at least until the big man here gets out of diapers. Penny's a terrific mom, much to her surprise, but I'm not pressing my luck."

"So what's the good news?"

"Molly's coming, at last. Finished her residency and a fellowship, and now she's as certified as can be. She had very attractive offers from existing practices both in Chicago and San Francisco plus a hospital in Dallas, but in the end, Sweetgrass did its magic. She decided to throw her lot in with Jake and me and set up her practice here, along with being part-time at a hospital in Austin. She said the baby boom in Sweetgrass would keep her busy enough until she could expand it to the surrounding area, and she's looking forward to being with family." Bridger shook his head. "I never thought I'd see my kid sister again, all those years ago. I'll never forget how it felt to see them taken away after that SOB who fathered us killed our mom." JJ was toddling off pretty fast, so Bridger picked him up and held him close, brushing over his child's hair with one big hand. "This guy and his siblings are never going to know the fear that filled our house." His jaw flexed. "I'd die before I'd harm a hair on their heads."

"Of course you would. You were just a kid yourself, Bridger." Michael clapped him on the shoulder, aware that he'd led a charmed life in comparison. He shouldn't be feeling bad now.

Laken would marry him someday, surely. "I'm glad about Molly. That's real good news for everyone here. How soon does she arrive?"

"Next week. I can't wait."

"I'll tell Laken. We don't have an OB yet—we'll be first on her appointment list when she's ready."

"We're working hard to get the equipment she wants to have. Doc Jake has great connections in Austin, and I'm a good scrounger. We can't run much longer without some help, though. A real receptionist would be amazing. Jake takes crappy messages, and I'm gone half the time as fire chief. We need to get our act together."

"Sweetgrass is really lucky to have you both, and Molly will be a great addition."

"Thanks. And hey, if I can do anything to help you with Laken…"

"If I had the first clue, I'd sure tell you."

It was Bridger's turn to clap Michael on the shoulder. "Sorry, man."

"Michael!" Laken's voice from behind him, urgent.

He whirled and took off as soon as he spotted her. "Are you okay? What's wrong?"

She halted, looking confused. "I'm an idiot is the only thing that's wrong. Michael—" She clutched his shoulders, then kissed him hard. "Michael, don't give up on me. Please don't give up on me."

"What?" He wrapped her in his arms. "What is it? What's happened?"

She looked into his eyes very seriously as tears brimmed. "Will you marry me at the community Christmas celebration?"

"What? But that's in just—"

"Three weeks," she finished for him. "I know. It's insane. But Jeanette will make my dress, and she says Spike has drawn up cake plans and Brenda has flower ideas and—" She caught sight of Bridger, who was gathering up JJ and trying to tiptoe off. "Bridger, will you barbecue for us?"

Bridger met Michael's gaze and grinned really big. "I would be delighted."

"Thank you," she said, then rose to her toes and kissed Michael again. "I'm sorry I've been so scared. I just don't want to mess up. I don't want to wreck your life or this baby's and I'm just so scared I will, but...you really love me, Michael. You really do, don't you, even though it makes no sense?"

He had no idea what was going through her brain, but then he seldom had. "It makes perfect sense to me. You're very lovable, Laken."

"I'm not. I know I'm not. I'm cranky and bitchy and hard to get along with and—"

"And sweet and kind and too honest for your own good—and blind to how great you are. To say nothing—" He stroked her cheek. "Of being so sexy I wish I could just lock us away for about a year together."

"I'll be fat soon. I won't be sexy."

"You'll always be sexy to me, Laken. When you're a hundred and three, I'll still be chasing you around the house."

"Promise?" Her eyes shimmered with tears.

"Cross my heart and hope to die." He followed suit with one finger.

"Don't say die. You can't ever die, Michael. Not ever."

He cradled her face in his hands. "Not for a really long time, Laken. And you can't either. But we'll just focus on today and love each other every second, okay? And when this baby comes, we'll have even more love in our home. We're going to have so much love in our lives, Laken."

"You're too good for me. You could do better, you know." She rose to her toes and cupped his jaws. "But don't you dare. You have not seen how mean I can be if any woman ever—"

Michael wanted to laugh but he didn't dare. Anyway, he felt like crying at the same time. "Laken, love. My only love. I'll never get over you. I'll love you to my last breath."

She bit her lip and more tears fell. "I'll do better. I promise I will. I'll be so good and sweet and easy you won't know what hit you."

"And then I'll be sad because some Stepford Laken took over the wild and unpredictable woman I love so much." He touched his forehead to hers. "Don't change, Laken. You're just right for me, exactly as you are."

She threw her arms around his neck and clung to him.

He wrapped her so tightly in his arms he wondered if she could breathe.

After endless moments, they put a few inches between them and he met her gaze again. "Christmas, really?"

"I'm insane, aren't I? We'll never get everything done."

"You're my kind of crazy, and yes, we will. But we'd better get started. Bridger, tell Laken your good news—"

He looked up but Bridger was nowhere to be found.

"What news?"

"It'll keep." He swept her up in his arms and headed for his pickup. "But this won't. We're sealing this promise the best kind of way, right now this instant."

"Here? In Bridger's barn?"

"Bridger won't mind."

"Michael, we can't—" His Laken, the saucy daredevil who'd try anything, sounded scandalized.

"Oh, all right, be stuffy, Stepford Laken. But you're not getting away from me now." He tossed her over his shoulder, and she squealed.

"Michael!"

He kept walking and focused on getting his woman home where he could have his way with her.

Or she could have her way with him.

Either was a win.

Chapter Six

No one in the Sweetgrass headquarters of Enigma dressed up, but Steph had today because—

She wasn't sure, exactly. Couldn't explain it even to herself. Some attempt, she supposed, to regain control of her life. To return to the footing she'd once thought natural.

But all she had to do was walk outside on the town square to know she wasn't in Kansas anymore, Toto. Actually she probably *was* in someplace as provincial as Kansas—but she was the witch with the flying monkeys, dropped down into the land of cowboys and barbecue.

"You all right, darlin'?" asked a very familiar voice.

No. No freaking way. Wyatt's crew wasn't supposed to start work for Jackson until—

Crap. Today was Tuesday. She was shaking her head as she turned.

And there he stood, Gavin O'Neill in the flesh. Looking far too delicious for her peace of mind in dusty jeans and beat-up work boots, a t-shirt that molded his fine upper body too well and…oh, man…a tool belt slung at his hips.

No fair.

"What?" he asked. But he was grinning as if he could read her thoughts.

Blast the man, he probably could. "Don't you have work to do?"

"And don't you make a picture?" he asked. "All slick and sleek and shiny."

Her spine went ramrod stiff. "I'm dressed for work."

His brows rose. "Jackson Gallagher has on a t-shirt and jeans."

"Jackson owns the company."

"You own your own portion. Does that make you a rich woman, darlin'? In need of a gigolo, perhaps?" He grinned as he opened his arms wide. "You could have both, your own personal man of all work and a love slave to boot. What do you say, sugar?" His eyes glowed with mischief.

She burst out laughing. "You're ridiculous. Go back to work."

"It's time for lunch. Would you prefer to have me escort you to Ruby's, or shall we have a picnic at the spring?"

"I don't eat lunch." Or she hadn't before she came to Sweetgrass, where Ruby and Scarlett fed her so well she was in danger of needing to let out seams.

"A pity." He clucked his tongue. "You need some meat on your bones, my mama would say."

"Do you actually have a mom?"

"I do, and she adores me the way you will soon." He took her elbow and began to escort her to Ruby's.

Steph tried to dig in her heels, but the man was ox-strong. "No. I'd rather not—" She wasn't up for the questions she'd get if they were seen together. Sweetgrass had a gossip mill that worked overtime.

"Fine, then. You can share my lunch."

"You'll need your strength. I—"

"Well, I have to admit I like the sound of that." His eyebrows waggled. One hand spread over his heart, and he patted it. "That gives a man a reason to live."

"You are such a jerk." But she laughed as she said it. "I'll grab something from Spike's cantina. You go on."

"Oh, no. I'd find myself eating alone, and that won't do.

Not when a much more tantalizing option has presented itself."

He followed her into the cantina Jackson had established for his employees. The place was open 24/7, since his geeks worked all hours, and when it wasn't staffed, Spike kept plenty of food in the coolers.

When they entered, Spike and Big D were arguing over which Marvel superhero was best.

"Oh come on, now," Big D complained. "Cap is just too white-bread. Give me some Black Widow any day."

Spike rolled her eyes. "Of course you'd like the black catsuit."

"You think Thor's long hair is hot. He's only an overmuscled egomaniac."

"You're just jealous."

"Superbrain here," he said, tapping his temple. "Brains beat brawn."

"And it's her…brains you admire? Not the boobs?"

"Oh come on—don't be a sexist. Nat is wicked smart. I'd think you'd like how kickass she is."

Steph went to the cooler and grabbed an apple and some yogurt. She turned back to get Spike to put it on her tab.

Gavin was buying two enormous cookies.

"I don't eat desserts," she said.

"Oh, you thought these were for you?" Gavin grinned. He turned to Spike. "Best add two more for my lady friend."

Spike's eyebrows neared her hairline, and she and Big D exchanged glances.

"I'm not his lady friend. We're not even friends."

"That's harsh, darlin'. Especially after that last kiss."

He turned and walked out whistling, leaving Steph spluttering an explanation. "We aren't—it wasn't—"

Spike and Big D were smiling and nodding. "Sure thing," Big D responded.

"Whatever, you ho," Spike said affectionately. "He's not

only hot but super-nice, Steph."

"I'm not—"

Gavin opened the door. "Grab us two waters, will you, sugar?"

"I—" Steph subsided, knowing he'd only keep making things worse if she didn't join him soon, and the two before her already had their minds made up. "Give me two waters," she snapped.

"Here you go...*sugar*," Big D chuckled.

"You can be fired," she said darkly.

"I can't," Spike piped up.

Muttering, Steph stalked to the door, then paused. "Personally, I'm Team Nick."

"Nick Fury isn't a superhero—" Big D protested.

"Of course he is," Spike argued. "He's the mastermind behind all the Avengers."

"You might as well call Agent Colson—"

Steph smiled to herself and left them arguing. At least they were off the topic of Gavin and herself.

She really wanted to give him a piece of her mind, but she was learning that the man was incorrigible. He wouldn't argue, he'd simply steamroll over her to get whatever he was set on having.

He picked up a heavy teak chair from the outdoor seating as though it were made of plastic. "I don't have a blanket, and I'm guessing you don't want to get your lady clothes dirty, sitting on the grass." He glanced down. "Don't your feet hurt in those skyscrapers?"

These were her favorite Jimmy Choos, broken in just right. "I wear heels a lot. I'm used to it."

"I don't see how." He set the chair beneath a huge old oak bordering the spring from which the town took its name. He seated her, then settled cross-legged at her feet, taking off his flannel shirt and spreading their picnic on it. Every movement made a different set of muscles flex beneath the form-fitting t-shirt. Good grief, the man made her mouth water.

She jerked her gaze away from the display before she could start drooling.

"Here—" He pressed a giant cookie into her hand. "Start with this. Maybe it will sweeten your disposition."

"What? You have some nerve—"

She faltered as he removed one shoe and set her foot on his thigh.

He began kneading with his thumb, stroking with his fingers, until she wanted to slide down in the chair, eyes rolling back in her head. "Oh, my…that's…" Lethal. Because not only did it feel incredibly good, but he also seemed to find a direct connection to other parts of her. Her nipples rose, and her body…yearned.

The hand with the cookie fell to her lap.

Gavin nipped it away before it could do any damage to her skirt. She saw him break off one bite with his fingers and put it in her mouth, then grab a second bite for himself before setting it aside to let his fingers continue their magic.

"Spike has a way with a dessert, doesn't she?"

"Unh…" Steph managed.

His soft chuckle slid over nerve endings already tingling from his touch.

"You can stop that in about a week or so…"

Another husky, sexy sound from his throat.

He electrified her, exasperated her, challenged her, made her smile…

Reel it back in, Steph. You can't afford to get involved.

A part of her mourned as most of her acknowledged the wisdom. She made herself sit up, removing that foot from his hand.

"Ready for the other?" he rumbled.

She opened her eyes and saw that he knew exactly what he was doing.

"Why?" she asked him softly. "Do you even like me?"

His bravado faded. "More than I should." Blue eyes met her own green ones.

"Gavin, there's no future for us."

"Maybe not, but can you honestly tell me you're not enjoying the present?" He removed her other shoe and began kneading.

She tried to pull back her foot, but he resisted. "Don't be foolish, darlin'. Your poor foot has suffered enough from your vanity."

And there he was again, the insufferable know-it-all. She crossed her arms over her midriff. "Fine. Service me, then—" She clamped her lips shut. What on earth had she just—

Gavin laughed, the rich, full rumble of a man who knew how to laugh, who enjoyed life, who understood joy. "Well, now, darlin', this foot massage may not quite meet that definition, but in a more private place, I say *game on*."

Mourning the loss already, she jerked her second foot from his grasp. "I hate you."

"If only you could." His grin was quick and unrepentant. "I have a lot to do and animals who won't like me being late to feed them before I come to fix your windows tonight. So settle down now, and let's eat."

"Settle—" She shrieked. "And you're not coming to fix my windows or repair my faucet or—"

"Faucet's fixed already, remember?" He shoved the cookie back in her mouth and began opening his own food, eyes sparkling as he watched her.

"You are so—"

"I know. That's what you like best about me."

There was no winning with this stubborn ox. It was a dilemma in which she'd never found herself before, unable to find a way to keep the upper hand.

"Oh, give me my yogurt and don't talk to me," she snapped.

Gavin only smiled angelically, then rose to his knees and kissed her before she could react. She fell into the kiss, even as she knew better.

It wasn't until he sat back after placing her yogurt in her hand that she could take a deep breath.

The next day Steph approached the coffee shop where she, Ellie, Ava and Laken's prospective mother-in-law Sophia were meeting to plan a shower for Laken.

Ava was already there, typing furiously on her laptop. Steph did not understand how Ava could block out all the noise and dive into her fictional world, but Ava assured her that she had a tougher time when everything was really quiet.

To each her own. Steph started to go order to give Ava a little more time, but Ava sat up straight, then tapped on her phone as if turning off an alarm. She looked around and saw Steph. "Hey, there. Right on time."

"You want something?" Steph asked.

Ava lifted her monster cup and shook her head. "I'm good."

After ordering her jet fuel, Steph watched the door while she waited to get her drink. Sophia wasn't that familiar with Austin, so she hoped the woman hadn't had trouble finding the place.

It was an illustration of how incompatible her worlds were. Sweetgrass was not an easy stroll from Austin. The trip took two hours—and that was if city traffic wasn't snarled as was usually the case.

She was the one who'd insisted on including someone from Sweetgrass, though. Laken had been taken to the town's bosom—first because Michael was roundly adored by the townspeople but eventually on her own account—and the town would want to be part of any celebration for the couple.

So Sophia had eagerly accepted when Steph had contacted her.

When Sophia entered, however, she brought a surprise with her: Scarlett had accompanied her. Scarlett was Michael's half-brother Ian's wife and a renowned chef who'd made her home in the tiny burg—something Steph still didn't quite understand.

Both of them smiled widely at Steph, dispensing hugs to her and, when she joined them, Ava, too. Sweetgrass people were big huggers. She was trying to get used to it.

"Well, this is a surprise," she told Scarlett. "I didn't think you were allowed to leave town."

Scarlett laughed. "Having two restaurants to run sure keeps me from traveling." Then she winked. "But I have a stealth mission besides the shower." Her eyes went wide. "Or was Laken teasing me about her favorite lingerie shop not being far away?"

Everyone grinned.

"Absolutely not," Ava said. "As a matter of fact, Tom would enjoy it if I paid a visit. Anyone else want to join us when we're done here?"

Steph would have expected Ellie to blush if she'd been present, but she was running late. Instead it was Sophia whose gaze dropped while her cheeks went fire-engine red.

Interesting.

Just then, however, Scarlett broke in and rescued her. "Sophia will have to come with me, of course, since we're in the same car."

Well, well. Michael's mother Sophia was living with Ian's father Gordon, her ex-husband, and speculation ran rampant in Sweetgrass about whether they'd marry again, but both Gordon and Sophia were maddeningly discreet.

You go, Sophia, she thought, and stepped in to help with Sophia's embarrassment. "So if you're both here, who's keeping Georgia?" Steph knew that Sophia pulled a lot of grandmother duty—with greatest pleasure.

"Gordon has her today," Sophia offered. "Though I'm fairly certain she'll be on a horse with her daddy at least part of the time. She's already horse-mad, and she's barely two."

"Oh, goodness," Ava said. "My daughter Siobhan went through a horse insanity period as a pre-teen. An expensive habit, that's for sure."

"Having a daddy with his own herd gives Georgia a leg up. But Ian's promised me she'll start with a pony when she's ready to ride on her own."

Sophia smiled. "However, she's already got her own filly, which Ian let her name herself."

A peal of laughter from Scarlett. "Registering a filly named *Blue Daddy* after Ian and his dog just about did Ian in. He said he'll never hear the end of it."

The love, the outrageous happiness Steph heard in every word was hard to bear—yet comforting, too. Even if you weren't a person to believe in happy endings for oneself, seeing evidence of them was still reassuring.

It was also why she couldn't stay in Sweetgrass Springs.

Yet seeing these two here in her new environment made her a little homesick, even if Sweetgrass wasn't her home. Nowhere was.

At last Ellie rushed in, and introductions were exchanged. Sophia and Scarlett ordered and promised to bring Ellie her drink, so Ellie followed Steph and Ava to a newly-vacated larger round table.

"Not like you to be late," Steph greeted Ellie.

"I need a wife," Ellie replied.

"Don't we all?" Ava asked.

"Why are you frowning at me?" Ellie asked Steph. "I'm not that late."

"I have a bone to pick with you, lady."

"With me?" Ellie's eyebrows rose.

"Yes, you. That man has been to my house three times

this week. He's fixed my faucet, my windows, and changed the lock on my door. He's driving me insane."

"What man?" Ava asked.

"Gavin," Ellie offered, grinning. "Has to be."

"Gavin?"

"Gavin O'Neill, remember? The big, gorgeous carpenter who works with Wyatt? Don't listen to a word Steph says. He's fabulous. Remember the beautiful doors on that last house Wyatt finished?"

Ava nodded. "Those doors were works of art, not mere wood. So why is this artisan playing handyman at Steph's loft?"

Steph made a rude noise.

"Are you talking about Gavin O'Neill?" Scarlett asked as she and Sophia sat down. "I haven't met him yet, but I understand he does a lot more than building houses. Do you suppose he'd make Laken a rocking chair?"

"I'm sure he would," Ellie answered. Then smirked. "Especially if Steph asked him."

"What?" Steph goggled.

Ellie simply smiled. "They met at Thanksgiving at my house, and Gavin's smitten. So is she."

"Smitten? Our Steph?" Ava asked.

"Ellie's lost her freaking mind." Steph glared at Ellie. "I am not smitten. The man's insufferable."

"But how is he in bed?" Ava asked. "You could certainly do worse than a strapping carpenter with good hands."

Steph fell quiet. Her reputation with men was well-known.

Ava stared. "Oh, my. I'm sorry. I would never have guessed…"

No one said a word in the awkward silence.

"Oh, all right," she snapped. "I don't know how he is in bed—are you satisfied now? The man kisses like a wet dream, but he hasn't done more than kiss me. Worse than that, he's told me he won't take things any further until I agree to reserve myself for only him." She snorted. "As if. I can't stand the sight of him."

Sophia and Scarlett exchanged glances.

"What?" Steph demanded.

"Nothing," Scarlett hastened to answer.

"Spike," Steph said darkly. "That town is a hotbed of gossip."

Scarlett grinned widely. "Speaking of which, did you hear about Michael and Laken?"

"Spill," Ava demanded. "What's she done now?"

"It couldn't be too bad. Bridger last saw them with Laken tossed over Michael's shoulder as he did the caveman thing."

"Oh." Ava patted her heart. "I love that stuff. It's my world."

Everyone laughed, and Steph felt better, having the spotlight off her. "So has Laken quit waffling?"

"Apparently. The wedding got moved up to the community Christmas celebration."

Steph blinked. "That's only three weeks away!"

Scarlett shrugged. "Apparently Jeanette cornered Laken and talked sense into her, and now she's making the gown, Brenda is working on flowers, Spike has a cake in the works and Bridger is barbecuing. Nana and I are working on the rest of the food, but everybody in town is chipping in."

"So what do we do about the shower?" Ava asked. "I had thought we'd combine the two, wedding and baby, but maybe we should delay the baby shower until after the first of the year."

"We could combine a bachelorette party with her wedding shower," Ellie suggested.

"Works for me," Ava replied. "What about the rest of you?"

Heads nodded. After sketching out a few plans and exchanging contact information, they had Laken's future well in hand.

"Now...back to Gavin," Ellie began.

Steph groaned. "No."

Ellie refused to be cowed. "Even at that first meeting, there were sparks flying between you. But I don't want him upsetting you."

"Upsetting me?" Steph snorted. "He's driving me crazy, is what. He's relentless and so blasted cheerful. And he's sexy," she growled. "I could just murder him."

Her friends exchanged glances.

"Steph, do you want me to have Wyatt talk to him?" Ellie asked.

"No, I do not." Steph regained control of herself. "The man I can't handle hasn't been born. He's just—different. Not good different, annoying different. I don't know why I've become his home improvement project, but he's got to run out of things to fix soon and then I'll ditch him."

Ellie stiffened. "Don't you hurt him, Steph. He's a wonderful man."

"How could I hurt someone who has the hide of a buffalo and the sensitivity of a rock?"

"Your eyes are sparkling, girlfriend." Ava's own eyes were eagle-sharp on her. "You're certainly not bored now, are you?" Then she glanced over at Ellie. Ellie grinned back, lifting one eyebrow.

"Just stop it, you two. This isn't funny." Steph tossed her head. "I'm not flustered. I'm furious."

Ava didn't try to hold back her own laughter.

Steph narrowed her eyes.

"I'm sorry," Ava choked. "Swallowed wrong." She quickly averted her face, turning the laugh into a cough.

Ellie carefully blanked her own face, but amusement lingered.

Scarlett spoke then. "I can testify from personal experience that the things a person fights hardest are often what she wants the most."

"That's right. You had to be surprised into marrying Ian, didn't you?" asked Ellie.

Scarlett laughed, unoffended. "I was so scared I couldn't do right by that man." She glanced at Sophia. "Much like Laken has been spooked."

Ava nodded. "If she hadn't wound up pregnant..."

"My son would have won out in the end," Sophia assured them. "Both of my boys have a way of getting what they want."

"Translation: they have heads hard as rocks," Scarlett said. But she was smiling. "Thank heavens. I bless the day that stubborn man set his sights on me. Now that Jeanette's come-to-Jesus chat with our Laken worked, she'll be grateful, too."

"She's mostly afraid she can't be what he needs," Steph said.

"She's lucky Michael is so steady," Scarlett replied. "He's one in a million. Kinda like his brother." She winked at Sophia, who smiled back.

"Gavin seems really...steady," Ellie offered, eyes twinkling.

"Bite me," Steph retorted. "Gavin is annoying. Bossy. Overbearing."

"And seriously hot," Scarlett supplied. "I got a glimpse when he made it to the café yesterday before he went home."

Everyone laughed but Steph.

Gavin was driving her crazy, absolutely determined to hold out until she made the promise she would never, ever make. Narrowing your options to one man was the first step on the road to delusion.

Some people weren't made for monogamy.

Steph was one of them.

"Don't we want to go ahead and plan the baby shower while we're here?" she asked, desperate for a change of topic.

Jeers and laughter were her answer.

Gavin missed a cut on the trim board. "Blast it."

"What's up?" Wyatt appeared beside him.

"I wasted this piece, and we're short enough on what we stripped and restored." He knew his tone was irritable but couldn't seem to help it. "Never mind. I'll figure out something."

Wyatt didn't move on, however. "You okay?"

"Dandy." Gavin eyed another piece he might be able to toenail together with this one… He shook his head brusquely. It wasn't like him to make such a mistake.

"You sure?"

"I said I'm—" Gavin exhaled in a gust. "It's nothing, really. At least, nothing you can fix."

Wyatt observed him, then began to smile. "Ten bucks the problem's initials are SH."

Gavin raked one hand through his hair. "Go ahead. Say you warned me."

"No need to rub it in. What's she doing?"

"You don't have enough time, I promise. And it's my own damn fault." But he settled back against the wall. "I'm a patient man," he began.

Wyatt chuckled. "The woman would try a saint."

Gavin's humor began to return. "This fish is going to take a very long line and a steady hand."

"You actually want to keep her? Steph?"

"Of course not. But she's fragile."

"Steph? The man-eater?"

"Don't call her that." Gavin's ire rose. "You don't understand her. There's a damaged child inside that shrewish woman." The more he observed her, the more he believed that. She was more scared than anything, and he wished he knew why.

"Shrew is a good description."

"Wyatt," Gavin said as cautiously as he could manage, "You haven't looked beneath the surface. A tender heart resides there. I'm probably a fool for wanting to be kind to that heart, but I do."

"Another one of your strays? I've seen your menagerie, watched how you slip food to the homeless guys and minister to my crew." Wyatt captured his gaze. "She'll chew you up and spit you out."

"She won't." Gavin shrugged. "And anyway, I didn't say I wanted to keep her, but she can't continue as she is. She's not happy. If she would only—" He broke off. "Maybe you're right that it's a fool's errand, but she gets to me. I am what I am, and I don't know how to turn my back on suffering. This one is like a wild cat who spits and fights out of fear. It takes time and patience to gentle them. Stephanie will need more than most."

"And in the end? Where is this headed?" Wyatt inquired. "You know Steph is violently opposed to the very idea of marriage."

Gavin recoiled. "I'm not looking to marry her—I'm not crazy. I want peace in my life, a woman with whom to live in contentment. You'd never have a day of it with Stephanie. It's just…" Gavin stared off into the distance. "I can't leave her this way. She needs to know there are men who can be trusted. That she can allow herself to be soft. She'll never be happy otherwise."

"Well." Wyatt shook his head. "You sure don't lack ambition." He clapped Gavin on the shoulder. "I admire you. I think." He grinned. "Or perhaps I should have you committed. Not sure which."

"Me either. Might keep the straitjacket handy. A little more time with her, and I may be ripe for it."

On the other hand, he thought as he watched Wyatt leave, *it might be time for a new tactic.*

A slow smile spread over his features as an idea struck him.

No guts, no glory, he'd been raised to believe.

On Saturday morning, Steph woke early, anticipating Gavin's arrival. Though she told herself he deserved her bed-head and no shower, she found herself dressed and ready, coffee dripping into the pot by eight o'clock.

An hour later, still no Gavin.

"He said he wanted to take a look at that squeaky closet door," she muttered. She contemplated going back to bed, but she wasn't sleepy.

She spent another hour picking up and straightening the loft, though her cleaning service would be in on Monday.

At ten-thirty, she broke. Punched in the cell number she'd told him she didn't want.

His phone rang and rang. At last he picked up. "Gavin O'Neill." His voice was distracted.

"Where are you?"

"Hmm—what?" Then his voice changed. "Why, hey, sugar. You're awake?"

She almost hung up on him. "You said you wanted to look at my closet door. How was I supposed to sleep, knowing you'd be barging in at the crack of dawn?"

"I was busy."

Busy with what? she wanted to ask but didn't. Her heart squeezed a little, and anger stirred when she realized she'd already become accustomed to him being around nearly every day.

"I might be able to drop by later," he offered.

"No need. The door doesn't bother me." *So there.* "Anyway, I have a full day." Though, she realized, not one item on her list held much appeal.

Which terrified her. "So, just…have a good day." She started to hang up.

"I was thinking," he said in a casual tone, "That perhaps

you might like to see my place."

"Your place?" she echoed.

"Yeah. I'm finishing a project. Since you have such a way with tools, maybe you'd like to lend a hand."

She could hear the smile in his voice and, curse him, that charmed her. "It's not nice to mock other people."

At last, that warm chuckle she'd come to depend on. "Oh, I wasn't mocking, darlin'. You do have a certain...manner with a tool in your hand."

Normally, Steph would assume a man saying that was talking dirty, but this was Gavin, and she could never quite be sure of anything where he was concerned. "So I could be, like, your apprentice?"

"Um...sure. There's all kinds of things I'd be delighted to teach you." There was an unmistakable grin in his voice.

"You *are* talking dirty to me, in that roundabout redneck way of yours, aren't you?"

"Me?" His voice was all innocence. "My sainted mama would faint to hear such a thing." The mischief in his tone grew even more pronounced. "Maybe you should come over and take my measure in person."

"You make me crazy, you know that?" She couldn't hold back her own laughter. This man—this impossibly aggravating, ornery, stubborn man—could make her, Steph Hargrove, giggle like the innocent girl she'd never been.

"Is that a complaint?"

"What do you think?" She found herself grinning into the phone. "All right, all right, give me the address. Maybe I'll drop by later," she said, deliberately using his casual words.

"Come soon, Stephanie." His tone edged into husky.

She shivered a little in anticipation as she wrote down the address and ended the call.

For a few moments, she stared out the window at a crisp, cool day that somehow seemed a little brighter.

Chapter Seven

Of course the woman would show up for manual labor wearing skinny jeans and a cropped tank that bared teasing glimpses of her smooth, taut belly, topped by some fuzzy sweater that probably cost the earth. On her feet were high-heeled ankle boots.

Gavin groaned silently. She would cost him his sanity, no question.

But oh, she did look delectable.

"You live practically in the country," she accused. She glanced around. "Your house is falling down, too."

Gavin couldn't help laughing. "Good afternoon to you, too." Then, unable to resist, he swooped in and placed a kiss on that sulky, sexy mouth of hers.

Stephanie sighed one breathy little moan, and it was all he could do not to snatch her up, to bear her inside and down on his bed. *Heaven help me.*

"I'll have you know that the exterior of my house is deceptive. The paint is only a primer until I figure out what colors I want. I have in mind a stained glass in that octagonal window above the porch roof, but I haven't yet found the right one."

He continued, "I've focused first on reinforcing the structure, then on making space livable inside. I will admit, though, that Wyatt believes I should have razed the entire structure."

He grinned. "But he'd be wrong. I found loblolly pine floors beneath ancient scarred vinyl, and there are crown moldings that were hand-carved."

She clung to her pose of nonchalance. "If you say so."

"Would you care to see for yourself?"

She hesitated. "You really like all this stuff, don't you? I mean—" She gestured around at his garden and the evidence of new trees he'd planted, shrubs he'd moved. "It's all kind of *Little House on the Prairie* or something."

"You a fan of Laura Ingalls Wilder?"

"You know who she is?"

He rolled his eyes. "There's more than one barn on my homeplace, but I wasn't born in one. I went to school. I read."

"Sorry." She shrugged. "I used to think they were kind of amazing. There was Pa and Ma and their kids, and they raised chickens and cows and—" She halted. "Well, anyway, you'd be right at home there."

He wove his fingers into hers and tugged her along. "This is how I lived back home. We grew our vegetables, my mama had hens for the eggs, Dad raised dairy cows. We all pitched in. With eight children, it was necessary."

She caught up with him. "Eight kids? Wow. I was an only child."

And didn't that loneliness shadow her?

"Which were you?" she asked. "Don't tell me—the oldest, since you're so bossy."

He grinned. "You'd be wrong. I'm the black sheep and square in the middle. An elder sister and two brothers, all raising families; two younger sisters, one married with a third baby on the way and one at college now. My two younger brothers are also bachelors but have at least stayed nearby, as my mama thinks I should have."

"At least they care."

"Your family isn't close?" The pain in her voice disturbed

him, and he wanted to know more.

She snorted. "I don't have one."

"No one?"

"My sperm donor left when I was little. I don't remember him." She looked away. "Unfortunately, my mother couldn't forget him. So she used whatever drug was handy until she found her way out of a life she hated."

"How old were you?" He was outraged on her behalf.

"Sixteen. It was a relief, really. Nothing I did ever fixed her."

"You had no other family?"

She shrugged. "It doesn't matter. I made it. I don't think about it anymore."

But she did, clearly, despite her bravado. Gavin's protective instincts surged. What had she endured once she was completely alone? What had her life been like before?

"They didn't deserve you," he said fiercely. When Steph didn't look at him, he took her chin and turned her face to his.

Her eyes widened. "You're angry," she marveled. "At them."

"Of course I am. You were a child, and you should have been cared for. Did you ever have a real home?"

"Lots of people don't, Gavin. You just…deal." She glanced around her. "Nothing like this, that's for sure." She met his gaze and laid her palm against his jaw. "But thanks for being upset for me." Her eyes were as soft as he'd ever seen them.

Upset? He was horrified. Furious because she was still so alone. He wanted to sweep her up in his arms and shield her.

Before he could, she turned away and studied his house. "So…explain to this city slicker exactly what you've done." Her tone made it clear she was done talking about the past.

He'd let it go for now. He already understood her well enough to know she wouldn't appreciate his pity. So he made himself turn his own attention to his house, but he didn't relinquish her hand. "Allow me to introduce you to my lifetime home improvement project," he gestured with his free arm. "Please place a donation in the jar by the door at the end of the tour, should you be so inclined. The homeowner is constantly in jeopardy of impoverishment."

Steph grinned up at him and managed a passable curtsy. "Do lead on, my good man."

"Certainly. But mind your step, miss." Though Gavin realized that the advice might more properly belong to him. What he'd learned still had him reeling.

And every glimpse of the heart behind the brittle façade made keeping his distance a little more difficult.

"So what about the project you mentioned?" Steph asked at the end of the tour as she stared at a piece of equipment Gavin called a router. She could barely imagine how the crown molding above their heads had come from this tool. Or what creating it had required. "Don't you need to get back to it? Should I go?" In truth, however, she was more intrigued than she'd expected. She'd never given a second thought to how a structure was built, much less that all the pieces hadn't come from some factory.

Plus focusing on this meant he wouldn't be asking her more about her past.

Or feeling sorry for her.

"There's time," he replied. "Want to see what I'm doing?"

"Why not?"

He led her outside to a frame building, a sort of garage that was also only painted with primer.

"So will the primer be enough to protect the house and this? Isn't the weather hard on them?"

"It is, but the primer will serve for now. I have to choose

my priorities. There's only me, and I don't want to borrow money, so I have to earn as I go. I'll need several days together to paint the place all at once, and doing so is critical to get the best effect."

"But it doesn't drive you crazy that everything's not done?"

"Anything truly worthwhile often needs patience."

"You have a lot of it, don't you?" She frowned. "I don't get that. My view is that you have to grab for everything as soon as you get the chance. You never know what will disappear and never come back."

He'd taken her hand again, and she found that she liked the sensation of his big hand swallowing hers. "Perhaps what's available for the grabbing isn't worth keeping," he said. "Slow is better."

Not to me, she was about to say when he opened the door to his—well, obviously not a garage. Tools of all sizes and descriptions were placed strategically around the floor or arranged on the walls. "Wow. What is all this?"

"The instruments of my trade. This," he indicated one that had a wicked saw blade sticking out of its flat surface, "Is a table saw. That is a band saw, and over there is a lathe."

"What's a lathe do?"

"Do you recall the missing balusters in the staircase? I'm replacing them with matching ones I turn on this."

"Really? How?"

He reached for a block of wood about three feet long and square. "I begin with this."

"I can't picture how that could become like the ones I saw. Would you show me? I mean, is it too much trouble?"

His eyes warmed. "Not at all. First put on these—" He handed her a set of goggles, then donned his own. "And these hearing protectors."

Once they were both armored, Steph's own voice sounded odd to her as she stepped up beside him and watched him fasten the long piece at each end. Then his hands went unerringly to a tool with a wooden handle and a curved metal shaft. On the end, it was rounded.

"This is a spindle gouge." He pointed to a spot on the other side of the machine. "You stand over there. This—" he indicated a flat metal edge he adjusted to come closer to the block "—is called a skew."

When Steph was in place, he flipped a switch and the wood began spinning. Gavin rested the handle of the tool at an angle on the skew. With deft hands, he leaned the tool in and out, and wood shavings all but leapt off the block in long curls. Beneath his hands began to appear graceful curves she could never have imagined creating from a block of wood.

"That's incredible."

"What?" He flipped the switch.

"Sorry." She stepped back, but she couldn't help wanting to touch. "I hope I didn't interrupt at a bad time."

He studied her and the hand that was rising by her side. "Come over here. You can help."

"Me? Oh, no, I couldn't—"

"I know you're curious, and there's no substitute for the feeling of the wood under your hands."

"But it's beautiful. I'll mess it up."

He shrugged. "I have more material."

She was torn between longing and fear. "I won't be good at it."

"Do you only do things you've already mastered? I think not. You weren't born an executive."

"Some would say I was born to be bossy."

"And there I won't disagree," he said with a smile. "Still, surely you've attempted the unfamiliar."

"I learned kickboxing," she admitted. "I'm really good at it—want to see?"

"Maybe later. For now, let's find out if there's a woodworker lurking within you."

"Okay." Truth be told, she really did want to try it. She assumed the place he indicated in front of him and tried to imitate his two-handed grip, one beneath and one over the tool, guiding it.

"Hold it firmly but keep your body relaxed." He arranged himself behind her, his big body both a comforting and disturbing presence. "You'll need to be both flexible and vigilant. No piece of wood is uniform throughout. Its textures and composition differ from spot to spot. Keep the spindle gouge slightly loose in your fingers, but clasp it carefully enough so that the turning doesn't dislodge it. I wouldn't want to see a scar in this lovely exterior of yours. Notice the edges of the tool. They're wicked sharp."

"Maybe I shouldn't…"

"Here, place your hands in mine, and we'll begin together so you can acquire a feel for this."

She fought past her awareness of his big, warm hands, of his hard body a shelter around her. She narrowed her eyes, staring hard and steeling herself.

Gavin kissed the side of her neck, jolting her.

"What was that for?"

"Don't tense up. Light on your feet, fluid in your motions."

Steph inhaled one good, deep breath. "Okay, I'm ready." *I hope.*

Gavin flipped the switch and drew her hands with his closer until the blade touched the wood. Steph gasped and jerked. The spindle gouge slipped, goring a crooked line in the wood before he pulled her hands back. "Sorry."

"You're doing fine. There's an entire forest sacrificed to my learning. Now relax against me, and let's begin again."

Relax. Against him.

Yeah, right. But she tried, and he was a good teacher. Soon her fascination was great enough to overcome most of her extreme awareness of his body touching hers. She focused and watched the curves form under her hands—

It was *her* hands doing this, she realized with a jitter. Gavin had let go, though he still stood right behind her, his body big and warm and—

Another crooked groove. "Sorry." *Focus, Steph.* She redoubled her efforts and moved the tool along the wood as she'd watched him do, weaving in and out and fashioning a curve not nearly as beautiful as his own, but not a total loss.

She pulled away and studied the piece still whirling in front of her. "Not bad, huh?"

Gavin leaned into her to flip off the switch. "Pretty damn good, in fact."

"For a beginner?" she asked, turning toward him.

His eyes were hot on her mouth, then flicked to hers. "Accept your due, Stephanie. You did well."

Though her insides jangled, her rush of triumph overrode them, and she had to smile, throwing her arms wide. "I loved it!"

"Careful, now." He plucked the instrument from her hand, but just as she would have retreated, he took a step toward her, and she lost her breath.

She hastened to cover her intense reaction to him. "Can I do another one?" Then she experienced a moment of unfamiliar shyness. "If you can spare the wood, I mean."

Those blue eyes saw too much. As happened so often, she had the sense that Gavin O'Neill understood her in ways that disturbed her.

Fortunately for her, he stepped away then, just before she could decide whether to yield to the kiss they were both obviously dying for or to run for her car before things got out of hand.

He turned back with another piece of wood. "All right. Let's try this one. It's oak, not pine. You'll want to pay attention to the difference in them." He went on to discuss those differences as he removed the turned piece and replaced it with the block.

And Steph couldn't decide whether to be miffed or relieved that she'd dodged that bullet.

"Why would you need a wife?" Steph asked much later after a delicious dinner. "You're a really good cook, too. What can a woman do for you that you can't do for yourself? I can't believe you actually baked that bread."

Gavin settled beside her in the porch swing, looking down at her with a knowing grin on his face.

"Well, sex, sure, but you don't need marriage for that."

He chuckled and rested his arm behind her. "Man was not made to live alone." He glanced over at her. "Woman, either."

"You're wrong. I prefer to be on my own." She lifted a shoulder. "Some of us just aren't meant for the long term."

Gavin smiled indulgently, then set the swing in motion with a shove of one foot. "For an intelligent woman, you don't make one lick of sense sometimes."

Steph elbowed him in the belly, but that didn't faze him.

"Protest as you will, sugar, but you know I'm right."

"I do not." She frowned and glanced over at him again as the feel of his belly registered. The man had a six-pack, she would swear. Suddenly she really, really wanted to see him out of that flannel shirt and the t-shirt beneath.

"What has that lovely brow so wrinkled?"

"You. You weren't supposed to be sexy, damn it."

"What?" He did a double-take, then guffawed. "How is one man supposed to keep up with that odd mind of yours?"

"You're big," she accused.

"I am. Exactly what am I supposed to do about that?"

"Nothing." She crossed her arms over her stomach and harrumphed. "My type is lean and dangerous."

Gavin sighed and set them swinging again. "You have no idea what your type is."

"I suppose you think it's you."

He captured her chin. "Why on earth would I want to make myself miserable, getting involved with a difficult woman like you? Last I looked, I hadn't taken leave of my senses."

Stung, Steph didn't respond. How could she argue? She was difficult. And okay, maybe sometimes she was tired of being so on edge all the time, but... He was so not her type, she reminded herself. A man who worked with his hands, who gardened and cooked. Who wanted some country girl type and had no taste for night life, for the dangerous edge of risk.

"What's going on in that serpentine brain?" he asked.

"Nothing. I should go," she said abruptly. "I never meant to spend the whole day here."

"Coward." His face was deadly serious.

"I most certainly am not."

He merely arched one eyebrow. "You know there's something between us, and you run rather than face it."

"Face what?" she scoffed. "You won't even kiss me. Who's the coward?"

His normally affable manner vanished completely. In a blink, he'd plucked her from her seat and settled her on his lap. Slid one big hand to cradle the back of her head.

And kissed the living socks off her.

For a second, she froze.

Then she dove in. To take control, she'd thought—but control wasn't in the cards. She dug her hands into his sides and felt muscles even more impressive than she'd realized. For all that Gavin looked stocky, he actually had great muscle definition. She'd had a fling with a bodybuilder once, and Gavin's torso and arms, not the product of steroids, she was sure, would have made that guy jealous.

Within seconds, she found herself surrounded by arms made of iron, snug against a big, warm body that felt like the haven she'd been seeking all of her life.

Gavin groaned and deepened the kiss, and Steph followed him into a special, private place she'd never visited...never even imagined. She slid her arms around his neck and pressed closer against him, wondering if she'd ever kissed a man before who'd taken her on such a rollercoaster ride of emotions, spanning the spectrum in seconds.

But she knew the answer already. There was only one Gavin. And she didn't know what to do with him.

Finally, it was Gavin who drew away, and Steph who whimpered and pulled him back. He resisted, though she felt his body's vivid response to her. He set her back a few inches, both of them breathing hard, then leaned his forehead against hers.

"Now, Gavin," she murmured. "Make love to me now."

Instead, he lifted her and set her on legs that wouldn't hold her, steadying her with his hands at her waist.

"No, sweetheart. Not in the heat of the moment."

"You want me. I know it, and you do, too."

"That's not enough."

"It's enough for tonight."

He looked at her sadly. "I'm beginning to think I want more than tonight."

"Do you always get what you want?" she whispered.

"I can't tell you. I've never wanted anything the way I want you. I only know that when we make love, it's not going to be a whim, not one of your flings. You're still not ready, darlin'. And I can wait. Not easily, damn you, but I'll manage."

Her body edgy and aching, Steph's temper spiked. She'd love nothing better than to stomp off and never see him again—except that wasn't at all what she craved to do with this excess of energy she was dying to spend in another fashion.

But he stood there looking at her, blue eyes sparking yet resolute, patient and seeing too much. Steph had a sense that she was fighting a battle for her life. He would change her. This couldn't last—they were too different—and where would she be then? Who was she if not Steph the Bombshell, with hot and cold running men?

"I can't be an Ellie, Gavin."

He smiled. "I happen to like Stephanie Hargrove, saints preserve my black soul."

She relaxed enough to laugh. "You are certifiably insane, you know that?"

He shrugged and turned away. "I'll make coffee."

Steph sighed. "It's a lousy substitute for sex."

"Ah, but that's where you're wrong, darlin'. Just consider it foreplay." He picked her up and strode inside with her. "Stay a little longer, would you?"

How could anyone remain angry at this man? She relaxed in his arms, enjoying an odd sense of freedom that the night would not, as so many of her other nights with men were, be about sex. He was the oddest person. He baffled her and enraged her... "Can I keep my balusters?"

He glanced down in surprise. "Of course." He didn't ask what she would do with them, didn't make fun of her for wanting them as souvenirs of a day she wouldn't soon forget. "With a little more practice, I'm betting you could turn one that would fit exactly on my stairs."

She blinked, absurdly pleased at the notion. "Really?" Then doubt crept in. "I don't think so."

"Then I have to believe for both of us." He seemed perfectly serious.

She stared at him and marveled at the kindness that was so integral to his nature. "What am I going to do with you?" she whispered.

He set her down on a bar stool in the beautiful kitchen he'd restored, trapping her between his arms and the counter, his eyes hot and blue and kind.

"Guess we'd have to take that journey to find out." He pressed a kiss to her forehead, then drew away with an obvious reluctance that pleased her enormously.

"I'd best be making that coffee now."

Steph swiveled to watch him, her greedy eyes following every move he made.

Chapter Eight

"No, you cannot wear your favorite LBD for your wedding," Jeanette said firmly. "Little black dresses are boring and predictable and not at all bride-like. Now strip and close your eyes."

"This sounds kinky. You're scaring me a little."

Jeanette snorted. Scarlett and Sophia snickered. "As if. Do it, and nobody gets hurt."

"I guess it's a little reassuring," Scarlett mock-whispered, "That Scary Jeanette hasn't been completely lost inside Nettie." Laken grinned at the name Jeanette's new daughter, Walker's six-year-old orphaned niece they'd both adopted, had given the woman she adored above all others.

"I'm not afraid of Scary Jeanette," Laken declared.

"Then you're the only one of us." Scarlett's grin was huge.

"Be afraid," Jeanette intoned. "Be very afraid. Your wedding is in my hands."

Laken pressed the heel of one hand to her breastbone. Truth to tell, she was terrified of everything these days. She had no clue how to be a mother, and the best man in the world didn't seem to understand that he was in the worst possible hands and—

"Uh-oh. Stop it, girls," Sophia ordered. She stepped up to Laken and placed one hand on her cheek. "Breathe, sweetheart. It's going to be okay, I promise."

Laken stared at the older woman, eyes brimming. "I don't think so."

Eyes soft, Sophia wrapped her arms around Laken and drew her head to her shoulder, patting her back as if Laken were the infant. "You trust Michael, don't you? My son is a good man."

"He's the best," Laken's voice cracked. "But I'm not. I'm so afraid I'll ruin his life." There. She'd said it.

Kindness radiated as Sophia shook her head slowly. "The only thing that would ruin Michael's life is to lose you."

Scarlett approached from the other side. And clasped her hand. "I thought I was all alone in the world before I found out that I had family in Texas, and even then, once I found Nana, I was so sure I didn't belong here." Her eyes went dreamy soft. "It's almost easier to keep being alone, isn't it? You can close up tight and stay safe. But love...love is the most terrifying thing in the world when you don't think you deserve it."

"I don't," Laken whispered. "I don't deserve him. He's such a good man."

"Would it help for me to tell you a few of his less attractive aspects?" Sophia volunteered. "Bring him down to size? Because he is just human, you know. Yes, he's got a big heart and he's very earnest. He'd give the shirt off his back to anyone who needed it."

Laken nodded, feeling worse by the minute.

"But have you ever noticed how he bangs his toothbrush on the sink? Or how he can leave a hundred pounds of hair in the bristles of his brush for eons? Or how he's a little casual with whether his underwear makes it into the hamper or under the bed?"

"Oh, man, I know! I swear that man keeps buying new underwear when he just needs to pay attention what he's got already—"

The other women were laughing, and suddenly Laken

could breathe again. "He's not perfect."

"He's not," his mother agreed.

"You don't have to be perfect either," Scarlett noted. "All you have to do is love him. You can do that, right?"

"Oh." Laken pressed her breastbone again, where her heart was too big for her chest. "I can't imagine not loving him." She made a face. "Annoyingly cheerful as he might be."

"I know, right?" Sophia beamed. "I could never be in a bad mood with him around. It's so aggravating."

Laken drew a deep breath for what felt like the first time in ages. "Thank you."

"So are we through trashing Michael?" Jeanette asked. "Can we get on with trying on this dress that's going to make his eyes pop out of his head?"

"Really?" Laken settled. "Gimme."

"Clothes off. Eyes closed."

Everyone knew you didn't change Jeanette's mind when she wasn't ready.

Laken sucked in a breath and pulled off her shirt, then shucked out of her jeans. "Okay, I'm ready." She squeezed her eyes nearly shut.

"I can see you peeking. Do I need to blindfold you?"

"Man, you're harsh." But her words were muffled as fabric slid over her head and down her body. It felt cool and sleek and so, so soft. "Can I—"

"Not yet," Jeanette snapped. A zipper at her back slid up, then a hook was fastened over the middle of her back.

"Oh…" Scarlett breathed.

"It's…perfect." Tears in Sophia's voice.

Jeanette fiddled a little at the hem, then at last she said, "Okay, open your eyes."

Laken did—and lost her breath all over again.

"Well? What do you think?" Jeanette snapped.

"I'm…it's…I look…"

"You don't like it." Jeanette stepped forward as if to unfasten the back.

Laken slapped her hands away, baring her teeth. "I am never taking this off. How on earth—Jeanette, you are a genius." Laken turned back and forth. "I need to see the back better." Even the three-way mirror didn't tell her all she needed to see.

"Turn around. There's another 3-way behind you."

The back was...low. But not bad-taste low. It hit just beneath her shoulder blades, then skimmed her waist so that the indentation she was starting to lose seemed as if she hadn't yet. Then it followed her hips and down her legs to her ankles in a long, fluid line. In the front, some sort of miracle kept it close to the lines of her body but not so much that her tiny-but-growing baby bump was showing. The bodice framed her breasts in a way that could have been provocative, but because of the palest sheer cream insert was tasteful. Pale lace more cream than white cupped her bountiful baby bosom. The entire gown was a shimmer of cream lace with red chiffon beneath, and it paid lip service to the flamenco dress she'd teased Sylvie about wearing. Done in a far-updated and classier version, a ruffle fell from between her breasts angling to the hip, then trailing in a curve to her hemline, drawing the eye away from her middle and adding a flair of drama she fell in love with instantly.

She pressed her hands over her mouth, and her eyes filled. "Jeanette..." She whirled. "I am never taking this off. Oh my sweet heaven...I look like...I look..."

"Graceful and sexy and ripe. You're a classy fertility goddess," Scarlett supplied.

Jeanette only smiled.

"Michael is going to die. His eyes are going to pop right out of his head," Scarlett said. "He's going to want to grab you and blow off the wedding while he carts you off to—"

She cast a glance at her mother-in-law, soon to be Laken's, too. It was almost like they were...

"Sisters..." Laken marveled aloud. "Scarlett...you'll be sort of my...sister."

"No sort of about it, kiddo." Scarlett clasped her hand, and Laken held on tight. Then she reached for Sophia. "And now I have—"

"A mother," Sophia supplied. "If you'll have me."

"Oh, I will...I want that so much. Good grief, what's happened to me?"

"Sweetgrass," Jeanette said, standing behind her, pride in her gaze. "Sweetgrass happened to you. Welcome to the insanity." Jeanette started laughing, and all of them joined in.

After a moment and hugs all around, Jeanette was all business again. "Okay, time to take it off."

Laken clutched her hands over her chest. "Do I have to?"

"You planning to hide here until the wedding?"

"Could I?"

Jeanette shook her head. "Something tells me Michael and Jackson both would notice your absence."

Laken did sort of want to just stare at herself in the mirror for another hour or two, then just hide away until all the hoopla was over.

Scarlett seemed to understand better than the others. "Once you get past the terror," she leaned forward to murmur. "It's actually pretty great to be the center of attention."

"And you know you've never minded that, girlfriend," Jeanette said.

Girlfriend. Sister. Mom.

Maybe this marriage deal had more to it than she'd realized.

"Two more minutes to soak in my total gorgeousness," she pleaded.

"Knock yourself out." Jeanette's smile was full of pride, well-deserved.

Somehow the backdrop of people who cared about her

made the gown look even better, Laken decided. "Oh, my Michael…watch out. I'm gonna slay you."

The others laughed, and the day felt bright, after all.

Gavin stayed away from Stephanie deliberately for nearly a week. He had much work to complete for Wyatt, thank goodness, and Scarlett and Ian McLaren had asked him to make a rocking chair for Laken and Michael's nursery.

He was also intent upon finishing the tiling in the master bathroom that was his concession to modernity. The original bath had been the size of a coat closet. He'd taken that space and a large chunk of the adjoining small bedroom and created a bathroom that would scandalize his family when they saw it. Their family of ten had shared one very basic bathroom and thought nothing of it. Their situation was typical for their valley.

One day they would understand that he was here to stay. Surely when he had a family of his own, his parents and at least some of his siblings would relent and pay him a visit. East Tennessee wasn't the wilds of Africa, after all.

Though, he had to admit, the prospect of a family seemed farther away than ever.

Because now there was Stephanie, who was distracting him from his chosen path.

Blast his pathetic soul, why couldn't he simply see reason and walk away from her? Yes, there was more softness in her than anyone else recognized, but the distance between that and Stephanie as a wife, much less a mother…surely the moon itself was closer.

What was it about her that drew him so? Was it, as his mother declared, only his weakness for the lost, the lonely? Stephanie was lonely, of that he was now certain, whatever she might argue, and she did want to make love with him very badly. How much of that, however, was simply her competitive urge? Had any man ever said no to her?

Why would they? Even a blind man, robbed of the sight of that tantalizing mouth, those endless legs, the sleek curves—that blind man would hear her husky, come-get-me voice and seek her out.

Yes, he wanted her to the point of distraction. But as lovely as her body was, it was Stephanie's spirit that captivated him. A quick mind, a wry wit, most of all, a wistfulness she normally hid well…there was much more to be discovered about her.

And he wanted to be the one to do it. Only him and no other.

But she had not yet forsaken her playmates, he'd learned. In a moment of weakness, he'd driven downtown and nearly parked his truck, ready to climb her steps and be done with the waiting.

Then he'd spotted her walking down the street, tossing her head coyly and smiling at another man, one whose expression clearly spoke of anticipation.

Damn you, he thought as he pulled into his driveway and parked. Finn came running, and Gavin wanted to brush past the dog, to throw something, to yell—

Horrified at the fury he felt and how that turned him into someone he couldn't like at all, Gavin exhaled in one powerful gust and dropped to his haunches. "Sorry, boy." He gave Finn a good rubbing, then let his head sag while the dog licked his cheek and whimpered.

Perhaps he wasn't up to the challenge she presented. Gentling Stephanie Hargrove required too much. She bore not the faintest resemblance to the woman he'd fixed up this house for, the woman who would make him happy.

Gavin rose and stared into the growing darkness.

And tasted the bitter ash of defeat.

He should give her the freedom she demanded, let her waste her life however she might. It was her life, after all, as she never ceased to point out, he thought as he strode toward his back door.

As he passed his shop, however, he couldn't help remembering her childlike joy in turning balusters, the shy pride when he'd said she could make one for his staircase.

He was so preoccupied as he ascended his back steps that he nearly toppled the package resting against his back door.

Gavin O'Neill was written on it in a bold yet feminine slash he didn't recognize. Beneath it, in smaller letters, *You don't have to like this, but I thought of you when I found it.*

Steph, it was signed.

He carried the bulky box inside, wondering how she'd managed it herself. He turned on the lights, then set it on his kitchen counter. What could the woman be doing? Carefully he slit the packing tape and dug through foam peanuts to a bubble-wrapped shape below.

Removing the mounds of cushioning required several more minutes, all the while his curiosity racing.

"Well, I'll be," he said to Finn when he reached the end. Gavin shook his head and glanced down at the dog. "She brought me a window."

It was the stained glass window he'd been seeking to place above the front porch. Nearly two years he'd been searching, not sure exactly what he wanted and determined to wait until he had that figured out.

You don't have to like this, she had written. He had thought he'd want to pick it out himself as he'd done with every last inch of this place up to now.

But somehow she'd known what he was looking for before he had. A Celtic knot, a lovers' knot in shades that would now determine his exterior paint choices at last—and all of them colors he liked.

Because she'd paid attention.

Perhaps she couldn't cook, didn't know a weed from a tomato plant, couldn't sew on a button. No, she wasn't an Ellie, as she was so fond of pointing out.

But somehow, prickly, difficult Stephanie Hargrove understood him. Saw into his heart.

"Oh, but I do like this, sweetheart, very much."

Just then the thought of the man he'd seen her with earlier punched a hole in the pleasure he felt, but he tightened his fingers on the window frame and knew that she'd never done anything like this for any of those temporary men.

Patience. *You have a lot of it, don't you?*

"I'll need even more, won't I, sugar?"

Slow is better, he'd said to her. "You ass," he chided himself. "Too cocky for your own good."

Then he had to smile. He'd made himself scarce, and she'd come to him—with a present, no less.

His normal optimism returned. "You're mine, sweetheart, and it's only you who refuses to see it." He shook his head. "Not that I have the first idea what to do with you."

Gavin studied his window with greedy eyes.

And couldn't help laughing. The woman would drive him around the bend if he let her, always so sure she could call her own tune.

But you might want to watch out, darlin'. This ole country boy has a few tricks of his own.

Chapter Nine

"Thank you so much for letting us get ready at your house, Ruby," Laken said as the older woman greeted her at the front door. "Especially when you and Arnie just got back from your trip to Branson."

"Think nothing of it, sugarplum. Being able to take a trip at all is still a miracle to me, and the way my nephew spoils me, traveling is almost too easy. Have you ever flown in Jackson's plane?"

"I have. Great, isn't it?" Laken struggled to keep up the patter, but her nerves were shot. "My dress is here?"

Ruby smiled and wrapped an arm around her waist. The tiny woman had a surprisingly strong grip. "Everything is going according to plan. Jeanette dropped off your gown, then ducked out for a minute to check on the courthouse, though I know Brenda has the decorations well in hand. Scarlett will be back from there any minute, and Sophia is—" She halted, glancing into her parlor. "Well, Sophia appears to be a little busy right now."

Laken peered over Ruby's shoulder to see Sophia and Gordon locked in an embrace. She grinned. "You kids...can't take you anywhere," she called out.

Sophia jumped back, her hands going to fiery cheeks. Laken realized they were wet with tears.

"Are you okay? Oh no—is it that you're sorry about the

wedding?"

Gordon pulled Sophia into his side and shook his head. "We couldn't be more delighted. This was just—"

Laken's brows flew. "I'm pretty sure we know what that was. And since I'm a big fan of doing that myself, I'm sure not going to criticize."

"No, you don't see—" Sophia's laughter wobbled. "I—we—that is, Gordon—"

"What she's trying to say is that I have finally convinced her to marry me. Or remarry me, I should say." His glance at Sophia was all adoration. "But this time, everything is different. And I'll make sure it stays that way, I promise." He never took his eyes off the woman in his arms.

Sophia had eyes only for him, too, and the love between them made Laken want to sigh. "I'm so happy for you. Michael will be over the moon," she said as she and Ruby crossed the room.

Hugs were exchanged all around.

Then Laken looked at Ruby. "Didn't I hear you and Scarlett got married at the same time?"

"That we did."

"You two should join us. It would be great."

"No—" Sophia was shaking her head vehemently. "No, that wouldn't be right."

Laken caught the wistfulness on Gordon's face. "You should," she said to him. "We'd be happy to share."

Gordon looked down at Sophia. They had a silent conversation, then with a small nod exchanged, they both smiled at Laken. "That's incredibly sweet," Sophia said, "but we want this to be your day. You and Michael should be the stars of the show."

Laken pressed one hand to her midriff. For once, her queasiness had nothing to do with the baby. "I'm not sure I'm up to that. Take the heat off me, please?"

Sophia placed one palm on her cheek, her eyes filled with

love. "It will be okay, I promise. It's pretty great, being the bride." she glanced up at Gordon. "Even if I made a mess of things after, I'll never forget our wedding day."

He smiled down at her. "Neither will I. And not just because I learned how much I hate wearing a tux."

"What I put your through, spoiled brat that I was," she said.

He bent to kiss her eyelids, one by one, then her mouth. "You gave me my son. And a lot of great memories. Now you're sharing a second son with me, and soon we'll have Laken and a new grandbaby. I have no complaints at all."

"You should have plenty. I wasn't—"

Gordon silenced her with a kiss. "Enough about the past."

Sophia smiled softly and turned to Laken again. "Thank you, more than I can begin to say. We would rather wait and have something small and quiet, just family—you're part of that family, you know," she said to Ruby. "And maybe a few friends, but we'll wait until after the holidays. We could even go do a simple clerk's office wedding by ourselves, but…"

"No quick, impersonal wedding, not for us, love," Gordon said. "I want to be with you until my last breath, so we're doing this up proper. But thank you," he said to Laken. "It's a generous offer, and we're grateful that you'd be willing to share your day."

She could see in him, despite the stroke that had left him with a permanent limp, the tall, strong, handsome cowboy Sophia had fallen in love with so many years ago. They'd been through heartache and spent half a lifetime apart. She hoped she and Michael would be able to avoid that sort of terrible rending, not that she wasn't sure they'd go through rough patches. She was too hardheaded not to drive him crazy sometimes. Though Michael had all the patience in the world, she knew she stretched it thin at times.

"You're very welcome. I should thank you."

"For what?"

"For about a million things, including your willingness to make me part of your family, but right this minute? You've steadied my nerves. Poor Michael...he's lost his mind to want me, hasn't he?"

Sophia's smile was fond. "No, he's the happiest I've ever seen him. A few nerves of his own, though."

"Really?"

"Mostly that you won't be there at the wedding."

"I may be neurotic, but I'm not stupid. He's the best man in the world, and I'm not letting him get away now. Too late, sucker."

Everyone laughed.

Then Sophia turned to Gordon. "Guess this is where we part ways. Go help my son—our son—get ready. I'll make sure Laken shows up." She winked at Laken.

But Gordon caught her arm as she was leaving. "Just a minute more."

Ruby grinned and Laken grinned back. "Come on, sweetheart. We can get started on our own."

Laken wanted to thank Gordon again before he left, but a quick glance backward showed that Gordon didn't know anyone but Sophia was in the room.

"Isn't that sweet?" She patted her heart and sighed. "I have no idea what's happened to me, Ruby. I've gone all mushy."

Ruby led her to the stairs. "Sweetgrass has happened to you, dear. That's the short and long of it."

Laken stopped at the foot of the stairs and turned to the little woman who'd refused to let Sweetgrass die. "Thank you for saving Sweetgrass for all of us. So many hearts have found their way home here."

Ruby hugged her. "You sure know how to make an old woman feel good, but I didn't do it by myself."

"Not the way I hear it."

Ruby's cheeks reddened, and she waved off the conversation. "Let's go get you into that beautiful gown. I'm going to enjoy watching Michael's eyes pop right out of his head."

"They'd better," Laken replied.

Laughing, they climbed the stairs.

Michael was tying his tie in the makeshift dressing room for the groom's party at the courthouse when he heard Ian's voice. A second later, his brother walked in, clapping Gordon on the back. "Way to go, Dad. That is awesome news."

Gordon's weathered face bore a sheepish smile. "Thank you. Uh, Michael…"

"Dad and Mom are getting married again—" Ian beamed. "Sorry, Dad. Should have let you tell him."

"Not exactly a surprise that you two are crazy about each other, Gordon." He crossed to the older man, hand extended. "But congratulations."

"You're okay with it, you sure?" Gordon asked.

"I'm more than okay. You and Mom want to do it tonight with us?"

Gordon clapped Michael on the shoulder. "Funny, Laken offered the same thing. Thank you, truly, but we'll wait our turn. This is your big day, you and Laken. We'll do something small, sometime after the holidays." He paused. "I have to admit, I'm relieved to know you don't mind."

"How could I? I've never seen my mother happier."

"I never stopped loving her. And the blame is on me, all of it. We should never have—"

"Let's not go there. The past is the past. I can't fully regret it, since I wouldn't be here if you hadn't split up, but I'm pretty sure she never really stopped loving you either, Gordon. She made a good life with my dad, but…I like who she is now. She's freer and more joyful. With you, she...blossoms."

"That means a lot, son." Gordon's voice was rough. "I know you're not really my son, but...it feels that way sometimes."

"You might not have been the man who fathered me, Gordon, but if Ian doesn't mind sharing, I know I'm real happy to have you in my life, too." He grinned at his brother. "And after this one here got past wanting to cold-cock me for simply breathing, he turned out to be pretty okay himself."

Ian grinned back. "Little brothers need to be smacked up the side of the head now and again, I hear."

"You didn't hear it from me." Then he grinned. "So what are we waiting for? I need to get my woman hog-tied before she makes a break for it."

"I got an advance glimpse of her," Gordon offered. "And if I had any heart pills, I'd give you one. You're gonna need it."

A thrill of pure desire zipped up Michael's spine. "She may be nervy and easy to spook, but there is no question I got me one fine-looking woman."

"Pretty sure your eyes are gonna roll right out of your head, but you'll just have to deal." Gordon clapped Michael on the shoulder. "Let's go get your girl."

With Ian and Gordon flanking him, Michael steadied the surprising flutter in his stomach and walked downstairs.

Laken waited outside the closed doors as her wedding party gathered. Sylvie was traveling again with Gabe but had insisted on giving Laken and Michael a party once they returned from Europe. The other Book Babe Luisa was here with her children and had stopped off to give Laken a hug. "He's a good man," she'd whispered into Laken's ear. "You deserve him."

Laken wasn't so sure, but she was absolutely positive she needed him more than air.

"Hold on a second—" Steph called out, racing toward them. "Here. You almost forgot this." She proffered Michael's wedding ring.

"Thank heavens!" Scarlett said. "I realized as we headed over that I'd left it on the dressing table. Thank you for going to get it, Steph."

"Amen, Steph—glad I didn't know," Laken said. "Good that you're here. Did Gavin come with you?"

Steph scowled. "No. Why would he?"

Laken shook her head. Sometimes Steph was way too much like her. She bent closer. "Please. Don't let your fear rob you of your chance."

"Chance for what?" Steph whispered back. "There's nothing to lose."

"There's everything." Laken gripped Steph's arm. "I know what it's like to think you can't do it, that you'll mess up a good man. But here's the thing about really good men, Steph: they don't break. They stick. Even when we're basket cases. He's good for you, Steph, and you deserve a good man."

Steph shook her head. "Alone is better for me. He doesn't see that I'm doing him a favor."

"Are you? Or are you letting fear win?"

Steph frowned. "I'm not. I just don't see how…"

"You may not be able to see. I couldn't. But Michael could, and if Gavin can, let him. Give love a chance." Her throat filled. "If I'd let my fear send Michael away, my life…it's an empty life, Steph, being too afraid to love. It's not safe, it's just…lonely. Please. Listen to your heart. And give his a chance."

"Laken? Are you ready?" called out Jeanette.

Steph stepped back. "Don't worry about me. I'm fine."

"You're not, but I'm going to hope he won't let you keep

running." Laken took a deep breath. "I want this for you, Steph. All of it."

Her friend looked at her as if she'd lost her mind.

But Laken knew better. She'd finally found her mind. And her heart. "I'm ready," she told Jeanette.

The doors opened, and Jeanette stepped out onto the aisle first, gorgeous in a maternity little black dress of her own creation, a single stem of bird-of-paradise bound into a striking bouquet that Brenda had created.

Scarlett stepped to Laken's side and kissed her cheek. "Here we go, Sis." She smiled and stepped out next. "Follow Mommy, Georgia, and stay close to Maisie, okay?"

The six-year-old went stiff with pride as she gripped two-year-old Georgia's hand, the two of them in black velvet dresses with white lace collars and cuffs, more white lace at the hems. In her free hand, Maisie held a white lace basket filled with the red petals they'd be dropping to mark Laken's path. As they walked forward, Georgia called out. "Mommy, see my petals?" With extreme attention, she dropped them one by one, then picked them up and replaced them if she didn't think they were quite right. Maisie rolled her eyes and gently urged the toddler to keep moving, but Georgia held firm.

The crowd tittered. Georgia was, in many ways, the child of the entire town, the sweetheart of all assembled. Much of the town had been present the night Scarlett had gone into labor and nearly died giving birth, Georgia in danger right along with her. So she held a special place in all their hearts.

Maisie tried for a distraction. "My daddy is singing, Georgia. Isn't he good?"

Country music superstar Walker Roundtree, as Sweetgrass tradition held, was singing while he and Henry Jones played guitars. Walker looked at Maisie and winked.

"Uh-huh," Georgia replied, reaching for another rose petal.

Laken couldn't help grinning. At this rate, she'd have time for a nap before her own turn.

Then Georgia's head rose, and she spotted Ian at the front. "Daddy! See me, Daddy?"

Ian, standing beside his brother, grinned. "I see you, honey. You're doing a great job."

Georgia turned to Maisie. "Let's go see our daddies, okay?"

"Georgia, we can't—" Maisie began.

But Georgia was not descended from two determined women for nothing. Maisie's words fell on deaf ears as Georgia took off running to her beloved father.

Ian chuckled and picked her up, pressing a kiss to her cheek and cuddling her close while Georgia nestled into his broad shoulder.

Maisie looked back at Laken. "Sorry."

"No big deal. Can you finish?"

"I can." Her shoulders squared, and she took over for her absent partner.

Laken's best friend Ava stopped in front of her and cupped her cheek. "I'm really happy for you, Laken. Michael is exactly as wonderful as you deserve. Be happy, my friend." Eyes shimmering and a fond smile on her face, she started her own steps down the aisle as matron of honor.

Don't you dare cry, Laken cautioned herself. But her heart was so full it could burst.

"Ready?" Gordon asked from beside her.

"Do I get to call you Dad?"

Gordon blushed. "If you want to."

"I want." She leaned her head against his shoulder. "Take me to Michael, Dad. I can't wait a second longer."

"Then we won't."

The music changed, the assembly stood and Laken entered on Gordon's arm, not at all sorry to see Michael's eyes pop wide when he spotted her. Then he grinned and patted his chest over his heart.

I love you so much, she mouthed. So much she could barely breathe.

Michael started forward, then halted.

"Might as well go after her," Jackson called out. "I went after Vee."

Laughter rolled over the crowd, and Laken wondered why she'd ever resisted being taken to the bosom of this amazing little town.

"Do you mind?" she asked Gordon.

"Not a bit."

So she let go of him and raced to meet the man she would love for the rest of her life.

When he swept her up, whirled her around and held her almost too tightly to breathe, she held him right back. "Thank you," she whispered in his ear, "For being smarter than me. For not giving up on me."

"There's nowhere for you to hide, babe. I caught you fair and square."

She leaned back and cupped his cheeks. "Not so fair. You blinded me with love. But I'm okay with that."

"Good." His eyes glowed.

"But maybe we should let Judge Porter do his thing now. And you might be wrinkling my dress."

"It's one hell of a dress."

"It really is." She bent closer. "Wait 'til you see what's under it."

"You're killing me." But Michael let her down gently, never letting go of her hand. "Let's do this."

She smiled up at him. "Let's do."

When they reached Judge Porter, he just shook his head. "Am I ever going to get to officiate at a normal wedding in this town?"

"Doubtful," Ian chimed in. "Do you really mind?"

"Not a bit. All right, you two. Behave for a minute now."

He cleared his throat. "Dearly Beloved…"

Laken and Michael barely heard a word.

But they never stopped looking into one another's eyes or holding hands until it was time for the rings. At last it was done.

"I now pronounce you husband and wife. You may kiss your bride," Judge Porter intoned.

Michael wasted no time.

"You're my best Christmas present ever," she murmured as he drew her into the kiss and the assembly applauded.

"And it's only Christmas Eve," Michael answered. "Imagine what Santa might bring if you've been a good girl."

Laken grinned wickedly. "Want me to show you just how good I can be?" Her eyebrows waggled. "And what's under this dress?"

Michael groaned. "You are evil." He grinned right back. "I love that about you."

He picked her up in his arms, kissing her as he carried her away, cheers and jeers following them.

Chapter Ten

On Christmas Eve after she'd returned from Sweetgrass to her place with as much haste as possible, Steph toasted Jimmy Stewart with her eggnog. "Here's to sappy movies, pal. You made the best." The joyous faces and uplifted voices of *It's A Wonderful Life* shone from her TV screen, and she wiped away a traitorous tear. "Idiot. What's wrong with you?" But as she hit the power button on the remote and the screen went dark, she knew. Not only was it Christmas, but Laken's wedding had had everyone on an emotional high. She'd had to get out of there.

She loathed Christmas worse than any other holiday. It was all about families, and every avenue to escape it was closed. No stores open, no clubs to lose yourself in music and dancing and whatever else might ensue that would help you pass the time until the world got back to normal.

There might be a bar open somewhere, maybe, full of people without families, but she just didn't have the heart to go look for it. She could manage one night, anyway. Not like she hadn't done it before.

She padded across the loft in fuzzy socks to get more eggnog. Halfway there, her buzzer sounded, and Steph glanced at the clock in surprise. Almost midnight.

The buzzer again.

She shrugged. "What the hell. Might as well see who it is.

Probably just some curious drunk." She hit the button. "We gave at the office."

"Now, sugar, is that any way to talk to a man bearing gifts?"

Gavin. "I'm not speaking to you. Go away." Where had he been while she'd been on pins and needles to know what he thought of her present? Giving him a window had been a stupid idea, hadn't she known that? "Why are you here at this hour?"

"Santa Claus has a lot of territory to cover. I just finished sneaking off Ellie's roof."

"You played Santa Claus for them?"

"I'm pretty sure that up there where you're warm is a better place to have this discussion, sweetheart. That is, unless you have company already." His tone went bitter.

"I should say yes."

"Open up, Stephanie."

"Don't call me sweetheart." But she hit the buzzer. "You better mean that about gifts."

"Would Santa be coming to such a good girl empty-handed?" Again the note of sarcasm.

But why should she care? Still, even Gavin in a testy mood was a welcome distraction.

She heard his footsteps on the stairs and yanked the door open. "Where have you been? Why haven't—" She burst out laughing.

The transformation was amazing. His powerful frame made an impressive Santa, but he was much plumper than normal. Friendly blue eyes gleamed at her above a snowy-white beard. He brandished a large package. "Nice to see you smiling, even at my expense."

Steph stepped back and let him inside. "What's padding you? You're not that big."

Gavin waggled his fake white eyebrows at her. "Good to hear you've been paying attention. And here I thought you only noticed my handyman skills."

She moved closer, but he stepped away. "Oh, no. No prodding and poking at St. Nick. Inappropriate behavior, Ms. Hargrove. Only good girls receive gifts."

The dark edge to his tone was gone, and his good humor was infectious. For the first time in nearly a week, Steph's heart lifted. "All right, spoilsport. So what's in the package?"

"What makes you think it's for you?"

"Uh-uh. You're too honorable. You'd never wave a package under my nose and then take it away. Now give."

"*Now give*," he echoed. "It's not Christmas morning, or barely that. This goes under the tree." He looked around the room, then back at her. "No tree?"

"A waste of resources." She jutted her chin.

"Not even artificial?"

One string of lights haphazardly draped over the bookcase. A couple of poinsettias. For the first time, she saw how sterile this must look, especially if he'd been at Ellie's.

"Never mind that. How about sharing a little of that eggnog with Santa?"

Steph glanced back at him, peering closely for any sign of pity. If it was pity, he'd be back out the door before he could blink.

He smiled and sat down on her big overstuffed chair, setting the package to one side and patting his lap. "On second thought, why don't you come sit here, little girl, and tell me what you want Santa to bring you?"

"Santa as a dirty old man. Now that's more my style."

Gavin shook his head, his gaze never leaving hers. "No, Stephanie. It isn't. Now come here and let me give you your present." He held out a hand in welcome.

She felt suddenly shy. "No eggnog first?"

"Not yet. I'm melting in this outfit."

More eager than she wanted to admit, Steph approached. She had no idea what could be in the box, but she couldn't resist the unexpected treat. "But I don't have a present for you."

"A little elf delivered one to my back door."

"That was a housewarming gift. Did you—never mind." If he hated it she didn't want to know.

His gloved hand turned her face to him. "It's a beautiful window, Stephanie. Perfect."

"So why—" She clamped her mouth shut.

"I needed to think," he said. "And I had something to finish. This is not the night to argue, sweetheart. This night the whole world brims with love. We'll talk more about the window, but for now, forget the debate and let me see your face when you open this."

At that moment, the child inside her that Steph had long assumed dead chose to make its appearance. Though she knew it was Gavin in the costume, that little girl wanted to sit on his lap and open the present she hadn't anticipated. A gift, in the purest sense of the word.

She pulled the box to her as she settled on his lap, feeling unaccountably shy but also supremely protected. Even more than she wanted to open the gift, she longed to cuddle against him, to lean her head on his shoulder and be a different Steph than the world saw every day.

Nonsense. She hugged the package to her as solemn blue eyes studied hers. "Am I too heavy?"

"Not a bit. I'm pretty sure I could be happy like this for a long while."

Inside Steph something eased, uncoiling when she hadn't known she was tightly wound. "We're so different."

"Yes." He nodded, his smile solemn. "That's us, sugar. The Odd Couple. But opposites attract, you know."

She didn't have a sassy comeback this time. "Are we? A couple?"

His gaze never left hers. "That's up to you. Me, I'm thinking yes."

"But why, Gavin? I'm—"

"Sh-h-h," he whispered, placing one gloved finger across her lips. "It's pointless to wonder why, sweetheart. I'll gladly talk for hours about what I love in you, but it isn't your head you should be heeding. It's your heart you should be hearing."

Love? No. "I don't let my heart call the shots, and you shouldn't. You barely know me."

"Ah, but you, my stubborn sweetheart, can't tell my heart whom to adore." He bounced her gently. "Now will you open this present before I expire from the heat?"

"Sorry." She was surprised to feel reluctant. Once she started opening the wrapping, it would soon be over, this special surprise. "Maybe I'll wait until it's actual morning, after all."

He shrugged. "You can wait…but I'm not leaving until I see your face." He stretched and yawned. "Best be getting the sofa ready, Stephanie darlin'. It's been a long day." But his smile was wide as if he was certain she'd crack.

She hugged it once more. "Thank you, Gavin. This is a wonderful surprise."

"So was my window." Pleasure beamed from his face. "I hope you like what's inside half as much."

For the first time, she understood that he was nervous, and somehow that settled her. She began to open it carefully.

"Hmmm. I always pictured you tearing into packages, ripping paper with abandon."

She shot him a glance, then grinned. "Oh, what the hell—you're right." She reverted to type and tore at the wrapping, eager to get inside.

Once she did, her heart stuttered. Lifting out the most exquisite wooden jewelry box she'd ever seen, Steph gasped, "Oh, Gavin—this is beautiful." She pushed the wrappings aside and settled the gift on her lap, running her fingers over the silky-smooth edges, the tiny golden hinges, the beautiful carving of a Celtic design with her name worked inside the coils.

She glanced at Gavin, who watched her closely. "I've never seen anything so exquisite. You made this, didn't you?"

He nodded solemnly. "Don't you want to look inside?"

"I do." Barely able to tear her gaze away from his, she started to open the lid, but it didn't immediately lift.

"Here, press this." His gloved hand was too big, so he bared it, then pointed to a tiny recess.

Steph marveled that those big hands could perform such delicate artistry. With trembling fingers, she pressed against the recess and heard a click. The lid opened slightly, and she raised it to peer inside.

She gasped. Delicate as the air, a slender golden chain rested on dark blue velvet, a heart worked in hammered gold dangling from it, a blood-red ruby nestled inside the gold. She lifted it in her fingers and watched it catch the light, then darted her gaze to Gavin.

Who looked less certain of himself than she'd ever seen him. She thought she liked that, and she smiled.

"Do you like it?" he asked.

There was no way she could tease a man whose heart was in his eyes like that. No matter how much it frightened her or what accepting this might mean.

But she had to ask. "What does this mean, Gavin?"

"It's only a little trinket, nothing special." But his eyes told the lie.

"Gavin, I..."

"Let's see how it looks." He shed his remaining glove, then took the necklace from her. "Turn around."

Steph obeyed, and he fastened it around her neck, then opened the top of the jewelry box wider so she could examine it in the mirror. The heart lay nestled just below the hollow of her throat, the ruby catching the light.

Gavin's finger traced around the heart, and his touch burned against her skin. Their eyes met in the mirror.

Steph swallowed, her mouth suddenly dry. "Gavin, I'm overwhelmed. The necklace...I've never had anything so delicate. And the box is incredible. I'm stunned that you made it for me. You shouldn't be building houses. You're an artisan. You could make a fortune on something like this."

"Maybe, but a fortune isn't important to me, darlin'. I don't want all kinds of people buying work I completed in haste to satisfy a banker. Money is not the measure, it's the pleasure in the eyes of the recipient that's my reward. The hours I spend are precious to me, and I will not invest them paying overhead or keeping my attention on the bottom line. This work is my joy, and it's enough for me to be present to see the reaction when my work is received."

"Did you see what you needed tonight?" She couldn't imagine the hours this must have taken.

He nodded solemnly, "I did."

"I'm glad, because for once in my life, words fail me."

He chuckled softly. "Now that in itself is a feat to trumpet."

"Want your thank-you kiss now?"

He shook his head. "I want out of this suit first." Gavin shifted beneath her.

"Wait—let me." Carefully, she laid the jewelry box on the side table. She removed his hat first, then his beard. Beneath them, his face was shiny with sweat, his shaggy hair matted down. She ran her fingers through it, lifting the strands and blowing through pursed lips to cool him. He closed his eyes and sighed in pleasure.

Then she began unbuttoning the jacket. "Good grief," she laughed. "No wonder you're sweating. Poor man—is this a down vest underneath?"

"I had to make it look authentic, and I couldn't gain fifty pounds in time."

She laughed, unzipping the vest, too, while he peeled off the eyebrows. She stripped the vest away but stopped in mid-gesture at the sight of his muscular frame clearly outlined by a sweat-soaked t-shirt. "My, Santa, what nice muscles you have," she attempted to joke through a throat that had tightened with lust.

She was touched to realize that Gavin was blushing, actually blushing. He leaned forward and pulled the jacket and vest from behind him and dumped them on the floor. When she started to rise, he used his other hand to pin her to his lap. "You're fine right there."

But she wasn't sure anymore. He'd played havoc with her heart for weeks now. The kisses they'd shared glowed in her memory like a beacon. And now he'd thrown gasoline on a fire with his gift.

She was so afraid he'd put her off again if she asked him to make love with her. She bunched her muscles to escape, but he stopped her again.

"So you're planning to renege on your thank you?" His gaze pinned her, suddenly angry and fierce. "Is it because of the guy you were with a few nights ago?"

"What guy?"

"The one with the black leather jacket."

"You were watching me? Spying on me?" She reached for the clasp of the necklace. "Forget it. Take this back. Take all of it." She leaped from his lap. "Get out."

He rose, towering over her. "I won't. I wasn't spying. I'd wanted to come see you because I missed you. But you were up to your old tricks, weren't you?"

"So what if I was?" But she hadn't been. She'd thought about it, yes, because she wasn't ready to make Gavin any promises they would both regret down the road.

"How can you do that?" His expression was thunderous. "You'd brought me a window, damn it, a perfect one. Then you went out with some asshole who's not worth half of you because you're frightened of what's between us?"

Not worth half of you. Even now he defended her. She had

to make him leave. She couldn't give in, couldn't let herself—
"I said get out. You don't know anything, you—you big jerk," she spat.

Those blue eyes speared into her, taking their time—too much time, damn him. Studying her like some bug on a pin.

Then a smile spread on his face.

"Don't you smile at me." She pointed at the door again. "I said go away. And take your gifts with you."

"You sent him packing, didn't you? But you won't admit that because you're scared. Come here." He took a step toward her.

She took a step back. "Don't touch me."

He didn't slow, and she couldn't seem to move. Then his big hand was on her cheek, and he was examining her too closely, seeing too much. "You fight yourself as much as me, sweetheart. Why are you so afraid for me to love you?"

"You can't love me, Gavin. Don't." She closed her eyes. "Please don't."

But it was too late. His lips were on hers. At first gentle and soft, easing hers into parting, then sipping, tasting with small, deadly kisses, each one destroying her resistance with their tenderness.

"Stephanie..." He groaned and drew her into him, that hard body that felt so much like a shelter in which she could hide. Could leave behind so much pain, so much sadness...

His mouth cruised over her face, down her throat, stealing the breath from her as his hands untied her robe.

For a second, she stirred, aware of how un-sexy her flannel boxers were.

"Sh-h. I'll never think of Yosemite Sam the same way again, sugar." His soft chuckle faded as his mouth danced a new and devastating glissade over her skin. He bared her body as he was baring her heart, walking her slowly backward toward her bedroom, then impatiently, gloriously sweeping her up into his arms.

I can't promise, she wanted to protest. *This won't last*, she needed to warn him because he was so good, so kind, so…

Sexy. Sweet heaven, the man was driving her out of her mind, taking time—so much of it, too much of it until she would scream—to tease at odd spots on her body, avoiding the clearly sexual and in the process, driving her up and up and up, his touch electrifying—

Steph crested with a cry. Soared and floated for endless moments as she marveled that he'd made her come without ever even—

"Oh, dear mercy…" Was that her voice so high and thin as his tongue swirled around her nipple? She felt his chuckle against her more than heard it. "Gavin…"

"Sh-h, sweetheart. Simply relax."

Relax? Then she realized that he'd stripped away his own clothes. Watched that big, hard, warm body cover hers.

Oh, how good he felt. How much she relished the sensation of him—she, who was nearly always on top. Who preferred it that way.

But Gavin was teaching her how little she knew as he continued his assault on her senses, devastating her every defense, dismantling them as though they were a child's blocks.

"Gavin, let me—" She was rising again as his fingers, his tongue, his heated breath… "Don't—"

"Again, sweetheart." His voice was warm honey. Darkest velvet.

"Gavin, I want you in—" Then all thought fled again as her body came apart, as she flew higher still.

But for once, she wasn't alone. Gavin kept her safe as she flew. She rode on thermals like a hawk, an eagle soaring into the crisp blue air, the beautiful and welcoming sky.

In the piercingly sweet aftermath, she floated back to earth. "Stephanie," he said, voice strained and taut now. "Look at me. Sugar, look at me."

Steph opened heavy eyes to see his blue ones wide open, hot and beautiful and fierce. "I love you, Stephanie Hargrove," he said, and before she could voice the caution she knew she should—

With a bold thrust, he joined them.

Steph's back bowed. Every cell of her body screamed with a freedom, a bliss she'd never before experienced. She was safe and she was flying and Gavin was with her and he loved her and—

Gavin found his release as she went sailing. Together they rode the night sky as one. Steph clasped him tightly, pressing every inch of herself against him in fear, in ecstasy, in demand, in longing and yearning.

I love you, he'd said.

I'm so afraid I might love you, too, Gavin.

But her heart wept, knowing she couldn't say it.

Because she could never love him as he deserved.

Gavin awoke with Stephanie's head pillowed on his shoulder. A slow, satisfied smile emerged as she whimpered at his movement, then curled more tightly against him.

Man, she was sweet. Would anyone who knew her recognize the woman who'd given herself up to him again and again in the night?

I have you now, my love. I know you as no one else does. Something very primal prowled inside him. *And they never will. You're done with playing around, sweetheart, whether or not you recognize it.*

He'd been voracious—they both had, their love play at turns tender and bawdy, each one surrendering, each one conquering. Greedy or gentle, fierce or flirty, Stephanie Hargrove was not what he'd thought he'd been waiting for all his life.

But she was what he wanted, heart and soul. He would, by God, have her. Though, he told himself with a wry smile, she wouldn't make it easy on him, of that he was certain.

She was his miracle, but that was not to say he expected prickly Stephanie Hargrove to magically turn soft overnight.

He chuckled quietly. Or ever, he hoped. Her spirit was half the appeal of her. She only needed showing that love was real. That he could be trusted with that frightened heart of hers.

Full of cheer and optimism, Gavin rose from her bed, energy coursing through him. He looked around him for clothing, then realized all he had was a Santa suit. *Didn't plan that out too well, did you?* He settled for his boxers, knowing the red pants would have to be cinched up in gathers where the padding no longer took up space, then walked into her kitchen area. Man, he was starving. Nothing like a good full night of loving to stimulate the appetite, was there?

A glance in her refrigerator had him sighing in dismay.

Right. This was Stephanie, after all. Well, surely she'd be hungry, too. He began a pot of coffee, then strode toward her room while it was brewing. For a moment, he simply stood beside the bed, enjoying the sight of her, all the hard edges smoothed off.

Prickly, yes. Quite likely always would be.

But enough gentling, and his cactus would bloom with the force of his loving.

For now, he was starving, and if he yielded to the temptation she presented, they'd be in that bed for hours yet, only to be found some time later, gaunt victims of starvation.

A shower, then. *Keep your hands off her, dude. Let the woman sleep.*

Gavin sighed and headed for the bathroom.

Sunlight filtered into the loft, a soft whistling barely audible over the sound of the shower. Steph frowned, then smiled and burrowed deeper under the covers as she remembered the night before. She missed the warmth of him, even as she groaned. Yes, Gavin was a morning person, apparently cheerful from the moment he awoke. She always had been, always would be, a creature of the night.

Night. Oh, such a night. Steph stretched in delight, recalling the hours just passed, the wonder of making love with Gavin.

I love you, he'd said. And not just once.

She sat up straight. No, it was too soon. Too… *Oh, Gavin. You think you love me, but…*

In the mirror across from her bed, the ruby at her throat winked in the sunlight. For a second, Steph let herself feel how much she wanted all of this to be real.

Even if she knew her limitations in a way she wished Gavin would never have to.

Oh, give it a rest. It's Christmas. The day she normally only endured suddenly glowed with fresh promise. They could take one day and indulge in the fantasy, couldn't they? Wasn't everyone else living in a dream world today, after all?

Steph sniffed the air as the rich scent of coffee drifted toward her. There could be real advantages to life with a morning person. Left up to her, coffee often had to wait until she got to the office.

Gavin's whistle stopped, replaced by song. Steph stretched again, then smiled. Wide. With an unaccustomed energy, she leapt from the bed and padded toward the bathroom. Moments later, she pulled back the shower curtain.

Gavin started at the intrusion of cold air, followed by her undoubtedly cold skin against his back.

She snuggled closer, warming herself against him.

"And good morning to you, sugar." Rinsing the soap from his face, Gavin turned his head to her, broad smile and dimples her reward. "Merry Christmas."

"Top of the mornin' to you, Tweety Bird."

He grinned, and she pressed her breasts against his back.

His response was instantaneous. He whirled and strong arms wrapped around her, lifting her up for a long, heated kiss, his body's reaction to her as powerful as it had been the night before.

Steph's own hunger answered. She wove fingers into his hair and twined one leg around his powerful thigh. As though she weighed nothing, Gavin pulled her higher, wrapping her legs around his waist. Pressing her back against the wall of the shower, he thrust inside her in one powerful stroke.

"Heaven help me, but I love you," he gasped, then stopped any protest with his mouth as he took her once more to the refuge only Gavin had ever shown her.

Steph's ability to think incinerated in the heat of her response to his hands, his lips, the feel of him inside her. Bliss roared through her veins and snuffed out all rational thought.

In the aftermath, Gavin held her tightly, his heaving breath against her throat triggering tiny aftershocks that sent goosebumps over her body. He was an assault on her senses, giving her both thrilling release and a sense of safety she'd never known. Steph tried to remember why she was bad for him, but she could only feel the pulse of delight through her body.

Gavin pulled back and grinned, his eyes still dark with passion but sparkling with good humor. "You have a way with a shower, Ms. Hargrove. I don't believe I've ever had my back scrubbed with fingernails before."

Steph was surprised to feel heat rush to her cheeks. She pulled away slightly.

"Don't," he admonished, refusing to let her go. "Don't ever be embarrassed with me, Stephanie. There's nothing forbidden to us, and it makes me feel great to have you lose yourself so completely."

His good humor was infectious. "As if your monumental ego needs any stroking," she complained.

Crooking one finger under her chin, he pressed a gentle kiss to her lips. "Ah, but you make a strong man weak, love."

Her mouth opened to put him on notice to protect himself, but before she could, he sidetracked her with one more quick, hard kiss.

"Now, my Delilah, let's get washed up. You don't have one decent morsel in this place, and I need my strength." He paused to waggle his brows at her. "As will you." His grin killed her, just demolished her. "We'll adjourn to my place, since there aren't any stores open. One of us, at least, has the sense to stock up on more than yogurt."

"I wasn't planning on company."

"But you had it, anyway, didn't you? Enjoyed it, too." His smile was smug.

"Some people just can't take no for an answer," she grumbled.

Gavin turned her under the cascading water and began to soap her up. "Someone wakes up grouchy, does she? Since I haven't yet done enough, apparently, to remedy that, let's see what tricks I might have up my sleeve."

"You don't have any sleeves. You're naked."

"Well, how about that? Pretty handy, yes?" Gavin's hands slicked over her body, teasing and taunting.

Steph laughed and set her own fingers to work.

Chapter Eleven

"Is there anything you don't do well?" Steph asked, prostrate on Gavin's sofa after devouring a trucker-sized breakfast.

"Let me think about it." A quick, slashing grin. "Nope."

She burst out laughing. "Careful you don't scrape that monstrous ego on the ceiling."

"It's not bragging if it's true, is it?" He lifted her feet and sat down, then resettled them on his lap and began rubbing.

Steph was pretty sure her eyes rolled back in her head.

"There was the one time when my sister Carol asked me to help her fix a dye job on her hair without Mom finding out what she'd done to herself."

Steph smiled. "And how were you as a hairdresser?"

He shrugged. "Was it my fault that I chose to be, shall we say, creative with the mixing?" His eyes twinkled. "Carol wound up with purple hair."

"You did that on purpose."

"So she accused. Me, I'd claim it as her just desserts after all the times I'd been forced to play silly girl games with her when I wanted to be out with my buddies."

"I'd bet you played games with her because you were a good boy."

"I'm pretty sure you just insulted me. I am not a tame rabbit." Then he chuckled. "Anyway, I'd like you to tell my mom I was so good. She'd probably hurt herself laughing. I was a wild kid, and that's a fact."

His eyes caught hers, and warmth spread through her, a sense of contentment she'd never before experienced.

It should scare the living daylights out of her.

In some ways, it did.

"What are you thinking, love?"

Love. I love you, he'd said in the heat of their joining.

Oh, Gavin, don't do that to yourself. I won't be good for you.

"Nothing."

"Somehow I doubt that." He lifted one foot and slowly peeled down her sock like a striptease. "But whatever put that frown on your face, let's see if we can change it." Never taking his eyes off her, he placed a slow kiss on her arch.

Steph's nostrils flared. She couldn't help squirming in delight.

"That's more like it," he said smugly.

"You think you have me right where you want me."

He waggled his eyebrows, then turned and began to prowl his way up her body. "Don't I?"

Steph closed her eyes. Drank in the feel of him popping the snap on her jeans, lowering the zipper, micron by micron. "You're killing me," she said.

He bent his head, nipped at the curve of her hip. "Now why would I want to do that, love?"

Love. "Gavin…" She had to warn him. "This is just…we're only…"

His jaw tightened. "Your litany grows tiresome, Stephanie. You care, I know that. I feel it. I see it in your eyes."

But I don't want to. Can't afford to. "But…" she began.

He hushed her with a kiss.

Just then, his phone rang.

"Crap," he muttered and melted her bones with another kiss.

Soon the phone stopped. He slid his fingers into her panties, and Steph moaned.

The phone rang again.

Gavin dropped his head. "It's my family." Blue eyes apologized. "I have to take it."

She found a smile. "I'll be right where you left me."

His own were serious. "Will you?"

She made her smile bright. "Are you kidding? I'm not done with you, lover boy."

He examined her closely, too closely, then shook his head. "I'll be back. Stay right there."

Then he was gone.

Steph felt too exposed, lying there half-dressed. Quickly she pulled up her jeans, refastened them.

Her sock, though, she clasped in one hand as if she could feel the warmth of him.

And transfer that into her heart.

"Yes, Mom," she heard Gavin say from the kitchen. "No, I haven't had Christmas dinner, but I will."

A silence. "No, I'm not alone. As a matter of fact..."

No. Steph tensed. *Don't do it.*

"There's someone special," he finished. "You'll like her."

Gavin, you can't...

Bits and pieces drifted in.

"She's a marketing executive."

"No, Mom. I doubt she wants to live in Tennessee. And it's too soon to ask." Exasperation. "Mom, you'll meet her when she's ready, not before."

Gavin, don't do this to yourself. To me.

A sigh. "I love her. That's all you need to know."

Steph jumped to her feet. Slipped on her shoes. Looked around for her purse, so she could get her keys and—

Gavin had driven her here in his truck.

She could walk. Or call a cab. Surely they operated on Christmas Day. But she hadn't brought her phone. She'd been so sated on sex she hadn't even noticed.

With mounting horror, she listened as Gavin exchanged greetings with others in his family, and she heard the homesickness in his voice. Cringed when she heard herself mentioned.

She had to make him stop. Right now, before—

"That's right, Dad," she heard. "There's someone special now."

A chuckle. "Not exactly. She's...maybe not what you wanted for me, but Dad, she's exactly what I want." Another pause. "No, she doesn't—I don't know. I'm working on it."

Steph chided herself for listening in, but someone had to look out for him. His family, who obviously adored him, lived too far away. They couldn't prevent him from making this mistake.

This *huge* mistake.

She had to break things off immediately, before he got more involved.

Because she couldn't bear to disappoint him, and she would. Not intentionally, no. If anyone had ever tempted her to give love a try, to forget all she knew about how it could go wrong, how unrealistic the notion was...

Gavin was that person. But it would come to no good end, and that big heart of his would suffer.

She was hardly an angel, and most times she didn't really care about the fallout of her actions, but—

This was Gavin. She had to be better, for his sake.

Steph watched him pace his kitchen, sometimes laughing, sometimes with the saddest expression on his face.

She wanted to run, without a word. But if she did, she was positive he would chase after her, the thickheaded fool. He brought new meaning to the word stubborn.

She would have to break his heart a little now so that later, she wouldn't break it more by not measuring up to his cockeyed vision of her.

She knew who she was.

But Gavin—stubborn, blind Gavin—didn't.

So she stood her ground and waited for him to get off the phone.

Gavin hung up and looked out the kitchen window for a moment, picturing them all there together, one big, messy crowd. The kitchen would be full of women and wonderful smells. On the porch would be his dad and grandpa smoking the smelly pipes that weren't allowed inside. Outside there would be children running around, dogs barking…

What he wouldn't give to be there in the thick of it.

And how horrified would the woman in the other room be if she could see it?

A wry smile curved his lips. It would be good for her, though. Stephanie Hargrove was the loneliest person he'd ever met.

He glanced at the clock. He'd been invited to the Prestons and knew she had, too. Though a part of him wanted her all to himself, they were her friends, and truth be told, being there would make up for some of what he was missing back home.

He turned and walked toward the living room. "We'd best be on our way if we're gonna make it to—"

She wasn't on the sofa where he'd left her. Where she'd promised to remain. She stood by the front door, stiff and waiting. "I need to go."

It didn't take a genius to know what had happened. "Eavesdropping?" He cursed himself for speaking his heart to his family. Hadn't he known she was far from ready?

"You weren't exactly whispering."

He leaned one shoulder on the doorframe, crossed his arms over his chest. "And I take it you didn't like what you heard?"

"I can't marry you. Why would you say such a thing to them?"

"Can't...or won't?" He kept his voice resolutely casual, his smile wide to hide his sinking heart. "Perhaps I should have waited—all right," he responded to the protest springing to her lips. "I definitely should have waited, but that doesn't change the fact of what's right for us."

"You are insufferable. You couldn't be more wrong."

He advanced on her. "Lie to yourself, Stephanie, but don't lie to me. There's something between us, something powerful."

She lifted one shoulder. "The sex is great, I'll admit."

"Don't you dare cheapen this by making it about sex."

"Damn you, don't do this." Her casualness vanished.

"Don't do what?" He straightened as well.

"Don't you ruin what's happened. I'm not ready to let you go yet."

"Who says it's your choice? I'm going nowhere."

"You have to now."

"Perhaps you'd care to explain that." He stepped closer.

She jammed a finger into his chest. "Back off. I warned you, Gavin. You can't say I didn't. If you refuse to listen and get hurt, it's not my fault."

Fury simmered. "Now who has the ego? You're so sure I can be hurt so easily?" Deliberately he kept his tone lazy and amused, though he was anything but.

"Don't you patronize me. I told you I'm not the marrying kind. Marriage is an obsolete institution. People who like each other, who have a good time, they get married and everything goes to hell from there."

"Ah." This was fear talking.

"Don't give me *Ah*. Look around you—divorce is everywhere. Marriage is a hidebound tradition that doesn't work today. People need to be free to come and go as they please."

Anger sparked again. "And being with me would diminish you somehow?"

She lifted her chin. "Yes."

"How?"

"That's not the point."

"What is your point, exactly?"

"I won't marry you, Gavin."

"I haven't asked you yet, have I? You're worked up over nothing."

"Worked up? Don't be insulting. Look, I don't want to argue. We're too different, that's all."

"Because I'm not hysterical?"

"Hysterical?" Steph jumped up and headed for the door. "I do not get hysterical. This conversation is over."

Over, was it? Be damned if it was.

In her outrage, she didn't hear his steps behind her. He closed the gap, swung her off her feet and slung her over his shoulder. "Do you think I asked to fall in love with you?" he growled. "You are a spoiled brat with no more vision than an old blind dog. You refuse to see what we could have."

"Let me down, you—you baboon." Steph pounded his back, wriggling and kicking wildly. "I hate you."

"You do not." Gavin dumped her on his bed.

She scrambled to her feet, and he stepped in her way. "Don't push me any further, Stephanie. You sit there and you cool off."

"You're insane. Haven't you heard one word I've said?"

"If I am, you've driven me there. Yes, I'm listening, but all I hear is drivel and fear."

"Fear? Me? I eat guys like you for breakfast."

He looked at the ceiling and prayed for patience. "Of course it's not men you're afraid of. It's yourself. Your brain, sweetheart, is your worst enemy. You think too much. Love isn't reasonable or logical. The heart doesn't care if it makes sense. The heart wants what the heart wants, it's that simple."

"The heart is only an organ that pumps blood. Everything else is self-delusion. People think they fall in love because they want to believe in that fantasy when they're afraid to be alone.

It's not real." She paused for a minute, and he waited to hear what would pour out of her next.

"Look, let's be reasonable about this. You and I are different, but we have a good time together. That doesn't have to go away if you can simply accept that's all this is. We can agree to disagree about sentimental matters."

He could almost see her in a business meeting, all cool logic, thinking that was enough.

"Now I'd like to go home, please."

"What about Ellie and Wyatt?"

"I'll just tell them I don't feel well." Her chin jutted. "It won't be a lie."

"This is a mistake," he said quietly.

"It is."

He was certain they didn't mean the same thing. "I won't come after you again, Stephanie. The next move is up to you."

Her eyes were huge and dark and serious. "It doesn't have to be this way."

"Relationships have to grow…or they die." Couldn't she see what she was doing to them? What they could be? "Don't act like a child." *Please.* But he was sick to death of being the only one to believe in them.

She watched him, and in her eyes, he thought he saw the stirrings of doubt, perhaps of regrets. "I wish I could make you understand," she said so faintly it was barely a whisper.

"What I understand is that you're going to let your fears win."

He saw her flinch from his words, but she didn't argue. Instead she put one hand on the doorknob. "Shall I call a cab?"

His heart was lead. "Very well," he said stiffly. "Suit yourself." He drew his keys from his pocket and reached past her to open the door for her.

The way, he thought bitterly, a man did for the woman he loved.

But he wouldn't beg for her to love him back.

Chapter Twelve

For the next three days, Steph worked like a maniac.

But she also checked her phone obsessively.

Gavin never called.

Well, that's good, isn't it? She asked her reflection in the gym mirror. *It's exactly what you wanted.*

The ache in her chest weighed a hundred pounds.

She felt like a kid who'd given away her favorite toy. She hadn't understood how much Gavin had brightened her life until he was gone.

But she was the only one who understood that this could only end badly. She'd had no choice, once he started spouting craziness like marriage, to end things before she inflicted damage he couldn't bear.

Because for all his great strength, Gavin's heart was soft and unprotected. She could live with most of what she'd done in her life, but she couldn't live with knowing she'd damaged that beautiful heart of his.

She'd done the right thing, she knew that. What she hadn't counted on was how much she would hurt.

And the only person she wanted to turn to for comfort was the one she'd had to shove away.

Steph ratcheted up the angle on the treadmill. She would get past this. She would sweat Gavin out of her system. She would get back in fighting trim, be back out in the game any day.

Ava stepped on the machine beside her. "Hi—Wow, what's wrong?"

"Nothing."

"Then why are you crying?"

Steph reached up, horrified to feel wet cheeks. "It's nothing."

"This is me, girlfriend. I can count the number of times I've seen you cry on...actually, I've never seen you cry. What gives?"

"I don't want to talk about it."

"It's that guy, isn't it? Gavin?"

"I don't know what you're talking about."

"Oh, lordy." Ava hit the stop button. Grabbed Steph's arm. "Come on."

Steph shook her off. "I'm busy."

"I don't care." Ava hit Steph's stop button, too, and practically dragged her off the machine. Once they were inside the locker room with no one around, Ava faced her. "Spill."

"There's nothing to say."

"Sure there's not." Ava studied her. She opened her mouth, then snapped it shut. Shook her head. "It has to be love. Nothing else makes a person so miserable. So do I need to kick his ass?"

"No!" Steph subsided immediately. "The fault isn't his, it's mine." Misery swamped her, enough so she made a painful admission. "I'm not in love. I can't be."

"Why not?"

"Because I'll screw it up."

"Why do you say that?"

"I can't make Gavin happy. He needs an Ellie. He deserves one, damn it. I can't be like her." Her chin jutted forward. "I don't even want to." But she knew she was lying. If she could be an Ellie, she would.

"Has he asked you to?" Ava sounded enraged. "Because

I'll march right over and read him the riot act. You're just fine as you are."

Steph sagged. "That's what he said."

"Then what's the problem?"

"If you knew him, you wouldn't ask. He's this cheerful giant who works magic with wood, who deserves babies on his lap and gardens full of flowers and some little cottage with hand-braided rugs on the floor. That's not me, Ava."

She began to pace. "I eat nails for breakfast. I party all night, Gavin's up with the chickens. I like bad boys and loud music. He talks like a damn poet. He's too patient, too cheerful. I'm bad-tempered and impatient, and I'm not going to change."

"Honey—" There was laughter in Ava's voice. "That's it?"

"It's not a joke. Anyway, it's over and just as well. We're completely ill-suited. I wear Armani suits and he doesn't even own a tie, I don't think."

"Ah, so you're ashamed of him."

"Of course not." Steph rounded on her. "I'm not a snob. I just…" Tears welled in the corners of her eyes. "I don't know how to fit him in, Ava. And I would screw it up, I know it. I'd feel like crap because he's such a good man, but I'd still do it. Sooner or later, I'd get restless and want to be out all night, and he'd be making hot chocolate and just want to rub my feet or something. He'd be miserable, and I would never forgive myself."

Ava put her hands on Steph's shoulders. "My grandmother used to call what you're doing borrowing trouble. Can't you just give this a chance? See how it plays out?"

"You don't understand. He came to my house dressed up as Santa and brought me a jewelry box he'd made himself. It's museum-quality stuff, Ava. And inside it was this necklace." She brought the piece out from beneath her old t-shirt. She should have taken it off, given it back…but she just couldn't.

Ava touched it gingerly. "It's exquisite."

"He kissed me and made my toes curl. Made love to me until I lost my mind. But then he told his family he was going to marry me."

"Well, then. He obviously deserves to be shot."

"It's not funny."

Ava rubbed her arm. "I can see that. What did you do?"

"I told him all the reasons why marriage is stupid."

Ava rolled her eyes. "Honey..." Ava stroked Steph's hair. "You're smarter than this. So have you seen Gavin since then?"

"No."

"Have you called him?

"I don't want to talk about this anymore. It's over, the end. For once in my life, I'm trying to be noble. Leave this, Ava."

"Just answer me one question first. How does he make you feel?"

Steph sighed loudly. "He's not just great in bed. He makes me feel so...cherished, so...special." Then she burst into tears again.

"And that's bad because...?"

"I'll ruin it. I won't mean to, but somehow I will. I'm not good at this, and Gavin deserves someone amazing." She shoved past her friend. "I don't want to talk about it anymore. Hard as it may be to believe, I'm thinking of someone else first for a change."

"Steph," Ava said. "Don't be an idiot. Don't walk away because you're scared."

"Too late," Steph whispered as she gathered her things to go. "I already did."

"Steph..."

But she rushed out before Ava could say more.

On New Year's Eve at the Preston house, Gavin strummed his guitar dispiritedly out on the porch after a fast-moving set he'd played for the assortment of guests.

It was a nice gathering of friends and neighbors where everyone danced and brought food, where friendship and community was celebrated.

He'd never felt lonelier in his life.

Not that Stephanie would fit in, he told himself. Oh, she cared enough about the Prestons to pretend she was enjoying herself, but this was not her type of gathering. Most likely she was in some hot, crowded, smoky club right now, gyrating that beautiful body with one nameless man or another, teasing them, letting them put their hands on her, draw her close when they hadn't the first notion of how to care for her—

He gripped the neck of his guitar, seized by an unbearable urge to smash it on the porch rail.

"Gavin?" A sweet voice from behind him. *Ellie.*

He exhaled. Eased his grip.

Stephanie had said they were too different. Thought that she could simply walk away, that she could discard his love like it was nothing.

Then be damned to you, Stephanie Hargrove.

A small hand touched his shoulder, and he whirled on her.

Ellie took a step back, and he was instantly ashamed. "I'm sorry." He set down his guitar and held up his hands. "I truly am—I don't—" Never in his life had he felt so out of control. So damned much pain.

Her eyes were soft and sympathetic as she approached him. "Are you all right? I saw you out here and you looked so…" She paused. "Is it Steph?"

He looked away, unable to stem a bitter laugh. "It's my

own fault."

"Why?"

"I—There's no point."

"Gavin…"

He steeled himself against her pity. "It isn't as though she didn't warn me, the blasted fool woman." His mouth twisted. "Though it's me who's the fool."

"Are you?"

He glanced back in surprise.

"She's scared, Gavin, that's all."

"I know that, but—" Again he shook his head. "She's also right. We're nothing alike. She would hate my life."

"Does she have to live it?"

He frowned. "What do you mean?"

"Does it have to be your way or hers?"

Gavin stared at Ellie. "The life she's living isn't good for her."

Ellie's head tilted. "So Steph's the one who has to change?"

He looked at Stephanie's friend, but he was really seeing Stephanie herself, remembering how she'd focused so hard on turning the balusters. How proud she'd been. "She would be happier."

But would she really? he asked himself for the first time. He thought about how little he'd questioned her about her work, how he didn't really know what she liked about her career or how she'd come to choose it.

And being with me would diminish you? he'd asked, so certain that couldn't be the case, that he was offering her something far better.

He considered his conversation with his dad on Christmas. *Son, only make certain that you respect the differences between you. Our way does not have to be yours.*

Hadn't he said that very thing to his family again and again? *I can't come back, Mom. I have a different life now.*

Yet he'd recreated most of his past life here in Texas, and he'd expected Stephanie to fit into it. He'd told her he didn't expect her to be an Ellie, but he'd never considered accepting her lifestyle for himself.

"She likes some of it," he defended himself. But how much of it would truly suit her? Was it only a changed Stephanie he wanted? His own image of who she should be?

"What time is it?" he asked Ellie.

"Just after ten-thirty."

Thirty minutes to get to her place. Less than an hour after that before midnight, and she could be in any number of clubs. Austin was a big town with endless venues for entertainment.

He wanted to be with her when the year turned. Needed to start the new year fresh, to tell her he'd been wrong, to see if there was a second chance for them.

Before it was too late.

Before her midnight kiss was with someone else, someone wrong for her.

And you've been so right for her?

He would be. Of that he'd make certain.

But where would he find her? How could he locate her in time?

"I have to go." He was desperate to find her before midnight. "Do you know her favorite clubs?" Shame on him that he didn't.

All he'd done was ask her to give up her life.

Ellie gave him two names. "They're both close to her place. I'll ask Ava and our kids. Someone may know others. I'll call if I learn more. Check your cell for calls, since the noise will be deafening down there and you might not hear the ring."

He raced for the door, then abruptly stopped. Turned and kissed Ellie's cheek. "Thank you. Wish me luck."

"I do."

"I'll likely need it."

She smiled. "That you will."

He smiled back. "Whatever it takes, she's worth it."

The music was hot and loud, just the way Steph liked it. The driving beat of the drums vibrated through her body, the wailing guitar notes sizzled up her spine. All around her, people were having a great time, anticipation high as the midnight hour approached.

A new year. Ergo, a new beginning.

Why did everyone always believe that?

Most people kept going in their same old tracks, year after year. Their lives were no different on January first than they'd been at the end of December. So what made them hope? Simple delusion?

Your brain, sweetheart, is your worst enemy. Love isn't reasonable or logical.

Steph halted in place, buffeted around by bodies on all sides.

Just answer me one question first. How does he make you feel? Ava had asked.

Don't let your fear rob you of your chance, Laken had urged her. *It's an empty life, Steph, being too afraid to love.*

Her so-called partner, a man she'd never seen before a few minutes ago, reached out to pull her close.

Steph recoiled. When his grip tightened on her waist, she turned and used her elbow to get free.

"Hey! What the hell did you do that for?"

She could barely hear him and knew she couldn't make clear what she didn't know. All she was sure of was that she wanted out of here. Now. She turned to leave.

"Hey, wait!" he yelled behind her, but Steph pushed her

way through the crowd, her agitation increasing with every step. Clawing her way out, she felt like she couldn't breathe.

Finally, she made it to the edge, gasping for air, her heart pounding wildly.

A lanky, pony-tailed biker appeared before her, eyes bleary. "Whassa matter, babe? Your date play rough? You can come with me."

She evaded his grasp and tried not to recall that once she might have gone with him. She had to get outside. Desperately. She couldn't think, could barely breathe, she needed—

Steph suddenly stopped, her mind catching up with the frenetic whirl she'd been in since Christmas.

Gavin. She needed Gavin.

Outside the building, she leaned against the wall for a second, stunned. She could have been with Gavin tonight, but she'd closed the door on him at Christmas.

Because he'd said he loved her.

Because he wanted her to say goodbye to a life of easy conquests and meaningless encounters.

Because he'd asked her to belong to him.

But how could she be sure she could make him happy? Sure, she could try to change. And she would, for Gavin. But she was thirty-six years old, and people her age didn't change, not really. There was a purity in his heart she'd tarnish, if she ever got too close. She'd accepted it long ago. Born to be bad.

So why didn't she go back to that club and dance the night away?

Because, she realized, she'd be less alone all by herself.

How she wished she knew where Gavin was right now, so she could call him, just hear his voice. Let him sweet-talk her with that silver tongue of his.

He might be at Ellie's. She could try to call, but first she'd have to get where she could hear. Sixth Street was mayhem, this close to midnight.

Her place was nearby. Steph began running, darting

through the crowd, skirting the drunks, avoiding the hands poised to grab.

Everyone wanted their midnight kiss. In years past, she'd shared many of them.

Every one meaningless.

Gavin, she thought. *I want Gavin.* If only she hadn't been so blasted stubborn. No, she wasn't right for him, maybe. And she didn't know how to believe in love.

But oh, how he made her want to.

How does he make you feel?

Amazing, she thought. Special. Like he can't see anything else when he's with me.

I love you, Stephanie.

Oh, God. What had she done?

"Hey, baby—" Someone reached for her.

Steph shoved him away, kept moving.

An ugly name followed her, but she didn't care.

Steph sniffled, then realized her face was wet with tears. Damn him, damn him, damn him. What a way to start the new year, acting like some lovesick calf over a man who was her polar opposite, who didn't even care enough to come after her.

She smacked headlong into someone. "Sorry—

Hands grabbed her. She shoved back.

"Sweetheart, it's me."

Her head shot up. "Gavin? What are you doing here?"

"Looking for you." But this was not the jovial Gavin she saw in front of her now.

"Really? Why?"

He only stared at her for a long moment, then drew her off to the side. He said something but she couldn't hear him.

"What?"

He glanced up impatiently, searching the crowded street. One big hand locked around her wrist, he towed her along until they reached the side street.

Halfway down the block, she dug in her heels. "Stop. What's wrong with you?"

He turned on her, his eyes anything but the cocky, cheerful ones she was used to.

"I should have listened to you."

"To me?" She went very still as the meaning of his expression sank in. *Here it comes. He doesn't love me. I've finally realized I love him just as he's accepted what I've been telling him about how wrong we are for each other.* Panic skittered up her spine. "Gavin..."

"What do you like best about your work?"

"What?" She stared at him in confusion.

"Tell me why you like marketing. Why did you want to work for Jackson?"

"Why on earth are you asking?"

"I don't really know you."

Irritation stirred, and it felt much better than fear. "That never bothered you before." She poked him in the chest with one finger. "I've said that again and again, haven't I? But you keep telling me you understand me better than I do." She stuck out her chin, waited for him to argue like always.

When he didn't, that scared her like nothing else. Her heart plummeted. "I don't want you to know all about me." She stared at her feet. "You won't want me then." And she wouldn't be able to bear it. She turned blindly to flee from the pain crowding her chest.

He grabbed her before she could escape. "What is it you want, Stephanie? Answer me that."

She didn't know this Gavin. He looked so weary, so serious. She longed to stroke his face, to run her fingers through his hair. To turn him back into the arrogant, cheery giant.

To cuddle against him.

She shivered at his distant manner. "What I want doesn't matter. You know I can't be your Ellie and—"

"I never asked you to."

She plunged ahead without listening. "—I would if I could, but—What did you just say?"

"I don't need you to be an Ellie. I don't even want you to be."

"But..." She frowned. "You're meant for someone exactly like that, someone who can do all those things like cook and garden and—" She burst into tears. "I'm not that kind of person. Damn you, I wasn't supposed to fall in love. I don't know how to be any good at it." She swiped at her runny nose. "This is all your fault," she blubbered.

Gavin reached in his pocket and brought out a handkerchief, wiping tenderly at her tears, then holding it so she could blow her nose. "What is?" he asked cautiously.

"That nothing fits anymore. That my loft is too lonely, that I don't want to dance with strangers, that—" She broke off at the sound of the crowd behind them chanting.

"*Ten...nine...*"

"Oh, no!" she wailed.

"What is it? What's wrong?" He moved closer.

"We—I—It's too soon!"

"For what?"

"I really, really wanted you to be my midnight kiss, but now everything's a mess. And *you*—you want to *talk* about things," she spat.

She thought she saw his lips curve a little but still he didn't speak.

"*Eight...seven...*"

Desperation took over. "You know what? I don't care. I *am* all wrong for you and you're not my type, but—but—too bad. I love you, Gavin O'Neill. Deal with it!"

He only stared at her, and dread ran roughshod over her fear.

"*Six...five...*"

"Okay, okay!" She threw up her hands. "I—I like the battle of wits, the puzzle of figuring out what consumers want.

And I—I went into business with Jackson because...well, I really don't know why. I believed in him and I was good at expressing his vision, at communicating with others. Not that you can tell that at the moment," she muttered. Then she glared at him. "Now would you please just kiss me?"

"*Four...three...*"

His lips twitched but still he didn't move. "You mean that? You love me?" he asked.

"Yes! What did I just say? Gavin, *please*—" Blast the man. Would he never—

She reached up to take matters into her own hands.

Before she could, Gavin crushed her against him, then laid on her a scorching kiss, one that was everything she'd ever hoped to feel of home and welcome and beginnings.

Steph's knees turned to water. *I didn't ruin it.*

She drew back to be sure. "I didn't ruin it, right?"

He smiled wide and clear as he shook his head. "You never had a prayer of escaping me, Stephanie."

"You arrogant—" She started to argue for form's sake, then thought better of it. They would argue again, probably often, but tonight...tonight was for lovers. For hope.

For new beginnings. And if that meant she was as delusional as she'd accused others of being, well, so what? Everything seemed possible now.

I'm listening to my heart, Laken.

With bone-deep gratitude for caring friends and stubborn men and second chances, Steph rose to her toes and tightened her arms around Gavin's neck. He picked her up and twirled her.

"*One!*" the crowd screamed. Fireworks crackled in the sky. Horns blared.

But Steph and Gavin were oblivious to anything but each other.

Far too busy laughing their way into midnight's kiss.

~THE END~

Thank you for letting me share my stories with you!

If you enjoyed BE MY MIDNIGHT KISS, I would be very grateful if you would help others find this book by recommending it to your friends in such places as GOODREADS, BOOKBUB and writing a review. If you would like to be informed when my next release is available, please sign up for my newsletter by visiting my website at www.jeanbrashear.com and follow me on BookBub.

Steph first appeared in this series in TEXAS REBEL, and she moved to Sweetgrass in TEXAS CHRISTMAS BRIDE (*holiday cookie recipes included!*) Laken and Michael's story began in THE BOOK BABES, while their love story is the heart of TEXAS HOPE. Sophia and Gordon's poignant story is part of TEXAS HOPE, as is Michael first meeting Ian, the brother he never knew he had.

The Gallaghers of Morning Star are cousins to The Gallaghers of Sweetgrass Springs, and their story begins with Maddie and Boone in TEXAS SECRETS.

Next up is COOKING KISSING AND COWBOYS, a fun and emotional romp featuring spunky pastry chef Spike and possibly the most unexpected man ever!

What is home, and how do you know when you've found it?

Gifted pastry chef Spike Ridley knows most everything about cooking, but the recipe for home has eluded her. Have mixer will travel has been her motto, and now she has lost the one person who'd loved her from childhood.

When she crashes—literally—into famed quarterback Tate Ransom, life takes an abrupt turn. Tate has suffered a deep personal loss of his own, and coupled with a career-threatening injury, the ground beneath him is shifting.

Forced into a road trip toward uncertain futures, the snarky sprite and celebrity jock get glimpses beneath the other's veneer, and what they find surprises them.

When Spike takes Tate to Sweetgrass Springs to hide out, the quirky town embraces him. Too soon his fame and the demands of his career catch up with them, and Tate faces a dilemma: to return to the glamorous life that feels barren, or to stay and fight for a future that won't mean anything if he can't make Spike see that she is already home in Sweetgrass—and he wants to share that home with her.

I love hearing from you, so please contact me through any of the options at the end of this book.

Thanks!
Jean

Please enjoy an excerpt from **COOKING KISSING AND COWBOYS:**

Thank the stars boarding was beginning. If he had to talk to one more person about The Hit, Tate Ransom couldn't guarantee what he'd say. His season was over, and he didn't want to rehash falling short on what was to have been the perfect season anymore.

He picked up the headphones that would give him a chance to hide and turned to enter his first-class row. Someone jostled him, and he turned too quickly on his beat-up left knee. His headphones went flying, and he heard a sickening crunch.

"Crap," swore the Goth teenager behind him. She looked over her shoulder at the man behind her. "Thanks for shoving me."

"You stopped too quick. Not my fault you broke your headphones."

"They're not mine." She pointed at Tate. "They're his."

The man glanced up, and his sour expression flipped to awe. "Oh, wow. Tate Ransom." He looked sick. "These are yours? Oh, man, I'm really sorry."

"What?" The girl spluttered. "You're sorry now but didn't care when you thought they were mine?" She glanced up at Tate and frowned. "Are you supposed to be somebody?"

"You don't know who he is?" The guy behind her goggled. "That's Tate Ransom, the Cowboys' quarterback."

"Rodeo guys need a quarterback?" Green eyes widened.

Tate's lips twitched.

"The *Dallas* Cowboys. Don't you—" The other passenger's glance scanned her head-to-toe black, lime green streaks in her messy dyed-black ponytail, then dismissed her. "Of course you don't follow football."

"Because I have a brain, you mean?"

The man was so outraged, Tate thought he might burst a blood vessel. Meanwhile the line was stacking up.

Tate summoned the patience he'd hoped to abandon for the next few hours. "No worries." He bent to pick up the pieces of his headphones just as she bent, too. Her skull collided with his with an audible crack.

She fell back, and he barely caught her before she took a tumble. She felt light as a fairy in his hands.

A flight attendant made her way through the crowd. "Is this person bothering you, Mr. Ransom?" She looked at the male passenger. "If you'll take your seat, sir, we need to board the plane quickly." Then she turned to the girl. "Please go to your seat, miss." She was already looking at Tate. "I'm very sorry, Mr. Ransom."

The teen didn't budge, arms wrapped around her backpack. The male passenger didn't move, either.

"The line's backing up, dude." She might be tiny, but she sure didn't lack for attitude.

"Go on," muttered the male passenger. "Head for your row."

"This is my row."

The man's eyebrows flew, and Tate's followed suit. "No. It isn't." He seldom flew commercial, but when he did, his assistant booked the whole row for privacy's sake.

"No?" Incredulous green eyes met his. "You don't own the plane."

"I don't share rows." He had to be alone. Had to be ready for what he would face. Coach was in trouble.

Coach Lloyd Stanley was the closest thing to a father he'd had. He owed the old man everything for seeing beyond a twelve-year-old's bravado into the scared kid beneath: no family, no home, no future.

But Coach had spotted something in him no one else ever had. He'd built a man from a scared, rebellious boy, and in the process, he'd made Tate's entire life possible, this charmed existence he led.

Coach couldn't be dying.

The girl hadn't budged, one slender brow lifted. She held out her phone and its boarding pass.

The flight attendant blinked. "Oh, dear." She turned to Tate. "She's right."

He could tell that in one quick glimpse at her screen. "Listen—" he read quickly "—Phoebe Ridley, I'll pay you double your ticket price if you'll move—"

"No. And it's Spike."

"Miss, would you come with me, and we'll straighten out—"

Head shake. "Nope." Her mouth wobbled, quickly straightened, and he realized she looked as exhausted as he felt.

"Folks, we really need to get this plane loaded," came the captain's voice over the intercom.

"Just...sit down, then." Tate closed his eyes and struggled for patience. None of this mattered. Only getting back to Coach in time did.

"Mr. Ransom, I'm so sorry. We'll comp your flight for having to share your row. Would you like a drink?"

He shook his head and dropped into his own seat.

"What about me?" Goth Tinkerbell asked. "Do I get comped for having to sit with the arrogant jock?"

Another flight attendant approached. "Jenny, the captain wants you. I'll take over with Mr. Ransom." She turned to him. "I'm Sheri, Mr. Ransom," she all but purred. "I'll be taking care of you today. What can I get you?" Her eyes said the menu was extensive. And could be more so.

"I'll take a vodka tonic," said the surly teen.

Tate's head whipped toward her. "You're underage."

She snorted. "I'm twenty-eight."

Tate blinked. "No way."

"Way."

"I'll need to see ID," said Sheri. "What would you like, Mr. Ransom?"

"Just water." And peace and quiet.

Phoebe settled into the seat beside him.

"Phoebe—"

"It's not Phoebe. I'm Spike."

"Of course you are."

"Look, I guess you're supposed to be important, based on all the suck-ups around here, but to me you're just another traveler, and I don't want to be here, I just want this trip done. This seat was arranged for me. You stay over there, and I'll stay away from you. And if you need some stupid headphones, take my earbuds." Eyes snapping, she held out a pair.

He shook his head, turned away and closed his eyes. "Just don't talk to me, all right?"

She snorted. "Trust me, that won't be a problem."

But for the slightest instant he thought he saw another flash of vulnerability. Surely not from Miss Snarky. He chalked it up to his own exhaustion, the after-effects of a blown game that cost the Cowboys their season, topped by the news that the only person in this world who really cared about him was dying.

"Fine," she echoed, slipped in the rejected earbuds and stared ahead.

Fine. Good. He pinched the bridge of his nose and wondered how to make the miles pass faster.

...Excerpt from COOKING KISSING AND COWBOYS by Jean Brashear © 2022.

THE SWEETGRASS SPRINGS Series in order:

TEXAS ROOTS (Ian and Scarlett)

TEXAS WILD (Mackey and Rissa)

TEXAS DREAMS (a reunion of all the Texas Heroes families)

TEXAS REBEL (Jackson and Veronica)

TEXAS BLAZE (Bridger and Penelope)

TEXAS CHRISTMAS BRIDE (a Texas Heroes reunion)

THE BOOK BABES (introducing Michael and Laken)

TEXAS HOPE (Michael and Laken)

TEXAS STRONG (Tank and Chrissy)

TEXAS SWEET (Brenda and Henry)

BE MINE THIS CHRISTMAS (Gib and Dulcie)

TEXAS CHARM (Jeanette and Walker)

TEXAS MAGIC (Dominic and Lexie)

BE MY MIDNIGHT KISS (Steph and Gavin)

COOKING KISSING AND COWBOYS (Spike and Tate)

About the Author

A letter to Rod Stewart resulting in a Cinderella 16th birthday for her daughter might have been the first step on Texas romance author Jean Brashear's path to being a *New York Times* and *USAToday* bestselling author of more than 50 novels in romance and women's fiction.

Jean's stories are hailed as "feel-good romance at its finest" and her quirky small towns are called "a special place for hearts that need healing." All are evidence of Jean's heartfelt belief that love is the most powerful force in the universe, and her stories reflect that bone-deep commitment to spreading her faith in the goodness that exists inside us all.

Connect With Jean

Visit Jean's website: www.jeanbrashear.com
BookBub: www.bookbub.com/authors/jean-brashear

To be notified of new releases and special deals, sign up for Jean's newsletter on her website

Made in the USA
Coppell, TX
22 October 2024